VITO LOVES GERALDINE

A Collection of Stories

by
JANICE EIDUS

VITO LOVES GERALDINE

First published by City Lights Books in 1990

Front cover illustration by Sara Schwartz
Design by Patricia Fujii, Sara Schwartz, and Amy Scholder

Library of Congress Cataloging-in-Publication Data
Eidus, Janice.
    Vito loves Geraldine, A collection of Stories / Janice Edius.
        p.   cm.
    ISBN 0-87286-247-X
    I. Title. II. Title: Vito loves Geraldine, A collection of Stories.
PS3555.I38V58   1990
813'.54--dc20

City Lights Books are available to bookstores through our primary
distributor: Subterranean Company, P.O. Box 10233, Eugene, OR
97440 (503) 343-6324. Our books are also available through library
jobbers and regional distributors. For personal orders and
catalogs, please write to City Lights Books, 261 Columbus
Avenue, San Francisco, CA 94133.

CITY LIGHTS BOOKS are edited by Lawrence Ferlinghetti and
Nancy J. Peters and published at the City Lights Bookstore, 261
Columbus Avenue, San Francisco, CA 94133.

This book, like the first, is for John Kastan.
And also for my parents.

ACKNOWLEDGEMENTS

I would like to thank The MacDowell Colony, the Corporation of Yaddo, The Virginia Center for the Creative Arts, the Edward Albee Foundation, and The Millay Colony for the Arts, where so many of these stories were written. And I would like to thank James Legg and Marnie Mueller for their support and wisdom.

Some of the stories in this collection first appeared in the following magazines and anthologies: *The Village Voice Literary Supplement*; *North American Review*; *Epoch*; *Swallow's Tale*; *Sequoia*; *The Greenfield Review*; *West Branch*; *New America*; *City Lights Review*; *Redstart*; *Groundswell*; *The Ark River Review*; and, *Atalanta: An Anthology of Creative Work Celebrating Women's Athletic Achievements*.

"To Boston" was a winner in the Redbook Young Writers Contest. "Vito Loves Geraldine" received an O. Henry Prize.

CONTENTS

Vito Loves Geraldine **1**

Davida's Own **22**

Robin's Nest **28**

The Dreaded Female Locker Room
  Talk **42**

Safe **45**

Just One Look **63**

Vanna **67**

On The Side of The Road **86**

The Flowers **97**

Shana. Sandy. Brenda. Lorraine. **103**

The Star-Crossed Love of Don Diego Del
  Perro and Chastity **109**

Fluent **120**

The Marriage of an Afternoon **125**

A Comb and a Snake **129**

The Resolution of Muscle **134**

The Country in Maura **140**

To Boston **150**

American Love Story **162**

"... well then you won't find much that *isn't* on the absurd side, will you? And yet, if you stop to think for a moment, there's a grain of truth in it. Whatever you may say, these things do happen—rarely, I admit, but they do happen."

—from "The Nose" by Nikolai Gogol

VITO LOVES GERALDINE

Vito Venecio was after me. He'd wanted to get into my pants ever since tenth grade. But even though we hung around with the same crowd back at Evander Childs High School, I never gave him the time of day. I, Geraldine Rizzoli, was the most popular girl in the crowd, I had my pick of the guys, you can ask anyone, Carmela or Pamela or Victoria, and they'll agree. And Vito was just a skinny little kid with a big greasy pompadour and a cowlick and acne and a big space between his front teeth. True, he could sing, and he and Vinny Feruge and Bobby Colucci and Richie DeSoto formed a doo wop group and called themselves Vito and the Olinvilles, but lots of the boys formed doo-wop groups and stood around on street corners doo-wopping their hearts out. Besides, I wasn't letting any of them into my pants either.

Carmela and Pamela and Victoria and all the other girls in the crowd would say, "Geraldine Rizzoli, teach me how to tease my hair as high as yours and how to put my eyeliner on so straight and thick," but I never gave away my secrets. I just set my black hair on beer cans every night and in the morning I teased it and teased it with my comb until sometimes I imagined that if I kept going I could get it high enough to reach the stars, and then I would spray it with hairspray that smelled like red roses and then I'd stroke on my black eyeliner until it went way past my eyes.

The kids in my crowd were the type who cut classes, smoked in the bathroom, and cursed. Yeah, even the girls cursed, and we weren't the type who went to church on Sundays, which drove our mothers crazy. Vito was one of the worst of us all. He just about never read a book or went to class, and I think his mother got him to set foot in the church maybe once the whole time he was growing up. I swear, it was some sort of a holy miracle that he actually got his diploma.

Anyway, like I said, lots of the boys wanted me and I liked to make out with them and sometimes I agreed to go steady for a week or two with one of the really handsome ones, like Sally-Boy Reticliano, but I never let any get into my pants. Because in my own way I was a good Catholic girl. And all this time Vito was wild about me and I wouldn't even make out with him. But when Vito and the Olinvilles got themselves an agent and cut a record, "Teenage Heartbreak," which Vito wrote, I started to see that Vito was different than I'd thought, different than the other boys. Because Vito had an artistic soul. Then, on graduation night, just a week after Vito and the Olinvilles recorded "Teenage Heartbreak," I realized that, all these years, I'd been in love with him, too, and was just too proud to admit it because he was a couple of inches shorter than me, and he had that acne and the space between his teeth. There I was, ready for the prom, all dressed up in my bright red prom dress and my hair teased higher than ever, waiting for my date, but my date wasn't Vito, it was Sally-Boy Reticliano, and I wanted to jump out of my skin. About halfway through the prom, I couldn't take it any more and I said, "Sally-Boy, I'm sorry, but I've just got to go over and talk to Vito." Sally-Boy, who was even worse at school than Vito, grunted, and I could tell that it was a sad grunt. But there was nothing I could do. I loved Vito and that was that. I spotted him standing alone in a corner. He was wearing a tux and his hair was greased up into a pompadour that was almost as high as my hair. He watched me as I walked across the auditorium to him, and even in my spiked heels, I felt as though I was floating on air. He said, "Aay, Geraldine, how goes it?" and then he took me by the arm and we left the auditorium. It was like he knew all along that one day I would come to him. It was a gorgeous spring night, I could even see a few stars, and Vito put his arm around me, and he had to tiptoe a little bit to reach. We walked over to the Gun Hill Projects, and we found a deserted bench in the project's laundry room, and Vito said, "Aay, Geraldine Rizzoli, I've been crazy about you since tenth grade. I even wrote 'Teenage Heartbreak' for you."

And I said, "Vito, I know, I guessed it, and I'm sorry I've been so dumb since tenth grade but your heart doesn't have to break any more. Tonight I'm yours."

And Vito and I made out on the bench for awhile but it didn't feel like just making out. I realized that Vito and I weren't kids anymore. It was like we had grown up all at once. So I said, "Vito, take me," and he said, "Aay, Geraldine Rizzoli, all *right!*" He had the keys to his older brother Danny's best friend Freddy's car, which was a beat up old wreck, but that night it looked like a Cadillac to me. It was parked back near the school, and we raced back along Gun Hill Road hoping that Sally-Boy and the others wouldn't see us. Even though Vito didn't have a license, he drove the car a few blocks away into the parking lot of the Immaculate Conception School. We climbed into the back seat and I lifted the skirt of my red prom dress and we made love for hours. We made sure I wouldn't get pregnant, because we wanted to do things just right. Like I said, I was a good Catholic girl, in my own way. Afterwards he walked me back to Olinville Ave. And he took out the car keys and carved "Vito Loves Geraldine" in a heart over the door of the elevator in my building, but he was careful to do it on another floor,

not the floor I lived on, because we didn't want my parents
to see. And then he said, "Aay, Geraldine Rizzoli, will you
marry me?" and I said, "Yeah, Vito, I will." So then we went
into the staircase of the building and he brushed off one of
the steps for me and we sat down together and started talking seriously about our future and he said, "Aay, you know,
Vinny and Bobby and Richie and me, it's a gas being Vito and
the Olinvilles and singing those doo-wop numbers, but I'm no
fool, I know we'll never be rich or famous. So I'll keep singing
for a couple more years, and then I'll get into some other line
of work and then we'll have kids, okay?" And I said sure, it
was okay with me if he wanted to sing for a few years until
we started our family. Then I told him that Mr. Pampino at the
Evander Sweet Store had offered me a job behind the counter
which meant that I could start saving money right away. "Aay,
Geraldine, you're no fool," he said. He gave me the thumbs up
sign and we kissed. Then he said, "Aay, Geraldine, let's do it
again, right here in the staircase," and he started pulling off
his tux, but I said I wasn't that kind of girl, so he just walked
me to my door and we said good night. We agreed that we
wouldn't announce our engagement until we each had a little
savings account of our own. That way our parents couldn't
say we were too young and irresponsible and try to stop the
wedding, which my father, who was very hot-tempered, was
likely to do.

The very next morning, Vito's agent called him and woke
him up and said that "Teenage Heartbreak" was actually going
to get played on the radio, on WMCA by The Good Guys, at
eight o'clock that night. That afternoon, we were all hanging
out with the crowd and Vito and Vinny and Bobby and Richie
were going crazy and they were shouting, "Aay, everyone,
WMCA, all *right!*" and stamping their feet and threatening to
punch each other out and give each other noogies on the tops
of their heads. Soon everyone on Olinville Ave. knew, and at
eight o'clock it was like another holy miracle, everyone on the
block had their windows open and we all blasted our radios so
that even the angels in Heaven had to have heard Vito and the
Olinvilles singing "Teenage Heartbreak" that night, which, like

I said, was written especially for me, Geraldine Rizzoli. Vito invited me to listen with him and his mother and father and his older brother Danny in their apartment. We hadn't told them we were engaged, though. Vito just said, "Aay, Ma, Geraldine Rizzoli here wants to listen to 'Teenage Heartbreak' on WMCA with us, okay?" His mother looked at me and nodded, and I had a feeling that she guessed that Vito and I were in love and that in her own way she was saying, "Welcome, my future daughter-in-law, welcome." So we sat around the kitchen table with the radio set up like a centerpiece and his mother and I cried when it came on and his father and Danny kept swearing in Italian and Vito just kept combing his pompadour with this frozen grin on his face. When it was over, everyone on the block came pounding on the door shouting, "Aay, Vito, open up, you're a star!" and we opened the door and we had a big party and everyone danced the lindy and the cha cha all over the Venecios' apartment.

Three days later "Teenage Heartbreak" made it to number one on the charts, which was just unbelievable, like twenty thousand holy miracles combined, especially considering how the guidance counselor at Evander Childs used to predict that Vito would end up in prison. The disk jockeys kept saying things like "these four boys from the streets of the Bronx are a phenomenon, ladies and gentleman, a genuine phenomenon!" Vito's mother saw my mother at Mass and told her that she'd been visited by an angel in white when she was pregnant with Vito and the angel told her, "Mrs. Venecio, you will have a son and this son shall be a great man!"

A week later Vito and the Olinvilles got flown out to L.A. to appear in those beach party movies, and Vito didn't even call me to say goodbye. So I sat in my room and cried a lot, but after a couple of weeks, I decided to chin up and accept my fate, because, like Vito said, I was no fool. Yeah, it was true that I was a ruined woman, labeled forever as a tramp, me, Geraldine Rizzoli, who'd made out with so many of the boys at Evander Childs High School, but who'd always been so careful never to let any of them into my pants, here I'd gone and done it with Vito Venecio who'd turned out to be a two faced liar, only interested in money and fame. Dumb, dumb, dumb, Geraldine, I thought. And I couldn't tell my parents because my father would have taken his life savings, I swear, and flown out to L.A. and killed Vito. And I couldn't even tell Pamela and Carmela and Victoria, because we'd pricked our fingers with sewing needles and made a pact sealed in blood that although we would make out with lots of boys, we would stay virgins until we got married. So whenever I got together with them and they talked about how unbelievable it was that skinny little Vito with the acne and the greasy pompadour had become so rich and famous, I would agree and try to act just like them, like I was just so proud that Vito and Vinny and Bobby and Richie were now millionaires. And after a month or so I started feeling pretty strong and I thought, okay, Vito, you bastard, you want to dump Geraldine Rizzoli, tough noogies to you, buddy. I was working at the Evander Sweet Store during the day and I'd begun making out with some of the guys in the crowd in the evenings again, even though my heart wasn't in it. But I figured that one day someone else's kisses might make me feel the way that Vito's kisses had made me feel, and I'd never know who it would be unless I tried it.

And then one night I was helping my mother with the supper dishes, which I did every single night since, like I said, in my own way, I was a good Catholic girl, when the phone rang and my mother said, "Geraldine, it's for you. It's Vito Venecio calling from Los Angeles," and she looked at me like she was suspicious about why Vito, who'd been trying to get into my pants all those years when he wasn't famous and I wouldn't give him the time of day, would still be calling me at home now that he was famous and could have his pick of girls. When she'd gone back into the kitchen, I picked up the phone but my hands were so wet and soapy that I could hardly hold onto the receiver. Vito said, "Aay, Geraldine Rizzoli," and his voice sounded like he was around the corner, but I knew he was really three thousand miles away surrounded by those silly looking bimbos from the beach party movies. "Aay, forgive me, Geraldine," he said, "I've been a creep, I know, I got carried away by all this money and fame crap but it's you I want, you and the old gang and my old life on Olinville Ave."

I didn't say anything, I was so angry and confused. And my hands were still so wet and soapy.

"Aay, Geraldine, will you wait for me?" Vito said, and he sounded like a little lost boy. "Please Geraldine, I'll be back, this ain't gonna last long, promise me, you'll wait for me as long as it takes."

"I don't know, Vito," I said, desperately trying to hold onto the phone, and now my hands were even wetter because I was crying and my tears were landing on them, "you could have called sooner."

"Aay, I know," he said, "this fame stuff, it's like a drug. But I'm coming home to you, Geraldine. Promise me you'll wait for me."

And he sounded so sad, and I took a deep breath, and I said, "I promise, Vito. I promise." And then the phone slipped from my grasp and hit the floor, and my mother yelled from the kitchen, "Geraldine, if you don't know how to talk on the phone without making a mess all over the floor, then don't talk on the phone!" I shouted, "I'm sorry, Ma!" but when I picked it up again, Vito was gone.

So the next day behind the counter at the Evander Sweet Store, I started making plans. I needed my independence. I knew I'd have to get an apartment so that when Vito came back, I'd be ready for him. But that night when I told my parents I was going to get my own apartment they raised holy hell. My mother was so furious she didn't even ask whether it had something to do with Vito's call. In fact, she never spoke to me about Vito after that, which makes me think that deep down she knew. The thing was, whether she knew or didn't know, seventeen-year-old Italian girls from the Bronx did not leave home until a wedding ring was around their finger, period. Even girls who cut classes and smoked and cursed. My parents sent me to talk to a priest at the Immaculate Conception Church, which was right next door to the Immaculate Conception School, the parking lot of which was where I gave myself to Vito in the back seat of his older brother Danny's best friend Freddy's car, and the priest said, "Geraldine Rizzoli, my child, your parents tell me that you wish to leave their home before you marry. Child, why do you wish to do such a thing, which reeks of the desire to commit sin?"

I shrugged and looked away, trying hard not to pop my chewing gum. I didn't want to seem too disrespectful, but that priest got nowhere with me. I was going to wait for Vito, and I needed to have my own apartment ready for him so the instant he got back we could start making love again and get married and start a family. And besides, even though the priest kept calling me a child, I'd been a woman ever since I let Vito into my pants. I ran my fingers through my hair trying to make the teased parts stand up even higher while the priest went on and on about Mary Magdalene. But I had my own spiritual mission which had nothing to do with the Church, and finally I couldn't help it, a big gum bubble went pop real loudly in my mouth and the priest called me a hellion and said I was beyond his help. So I got up and left, pulling the pieces of gum off my lips.

The priest told my father that the only solution was to chain me up in my bedroom. But my mother and father, bless their hearts, may have been Catholic and Italian and hot tempered, but they were good people, so instead they got my father's best friend, Pop Giordano, who'd been like an uncle to me ever since I was in diapers, to rent me an apartment in the building he owned. And the building just happened to be on Olinville Ave., right next door to my parents' building. So they were happy enough. I insisted on a two bedroom right from the start so that Vito wouldn't feel cramped when he came back, not that I told them why I needed that much room. "A two bedroom," my mother kept repeating. "Suddenly my daughter is such a grown up she wants a two bedroom!"

So Pop gave me the biggest two bedroom in the building and I moved in, and Pop promised my father to let him know if I kept late hours, and my father said he'd kill me if I did, but I wasn't worried about that. My days of making out with the boys of Olinville Ave. were over. I would wait for Vito, and I would live like a nun until he returned to me.

My mother even ended up helping me decorate the apartment, and to make her happy I hung a velour painting of Jesus above the sofa in the living room. I didn't think Vito would mind too much since his mother had one in her living room too. I didn't intend to call Vito or write him to give him my new address. He'd be back soon enough and he'd figure out where I was.

And I began to wait. But a couple of weeks after I moved into the apartment I couldn't take not telling anyone. I felt like I'd scream or do something crazy if I didn't confide in someone. So I told Pop. Pop wore shiny black suits and black shirts with white ties and a big diamond ring on his pinky finger and he didn't have a steady job like my father who delivered hot dogs by truck to restaurants all over the Bronx, or like Vito's father who was a construction worker. I figured that if anyone knew the way the world worked, it was Pop. He promised he'd never tell, and he twirled his black mustache and said, "Geraldine Rizzoli, you're like my own daughter, like my flesh and blood, and I'm sorry you lost your cherry before you got married but if you want to wait for Vito, wait."

So I settled in to my new life and I waited. That was the period that Vito kept turning out hit songs and making beach party movies and I'd hear him interviewed on the radio and he never sounded like the Vito I knew. It sounded like someone else had written his words for him. He'd get all corny and sentimental about the Bronx, and about how his heart was still there, and he'd say all these sappy things about the fish market on the corner of Olinville Ave., but that was such crap, because Vito never shopped for food. His mother did all the shopping, Vito wouldn't be caught dead in the Olinville fish market, except maybe to mooch a cigarette off of Carmine Casella, who worked behind the counter. Vito didn't even like fish. And I felt sad and worried for him. He'd become a kind of doo-wop robot, he and the Olinvilles, mouthing other people's words. I noticed that he'd even stopped writing songs after "Teenage Heartbreak." Sometimes I could hardly stand waiting for him. But on Olinville Ave., a promise was a promise. People had

been found floating face down in the Bronx River for breaking smaller promises than that. Besides, I still loved Vito.

Pamela married Johnny Ciccarone, Carmela married
Ricky Giampino, and Victoria married Sidney Goldberg, from
the Special Progress Accelerated class, which was a big surprise, and they all got apartments in the neighborhood. But after a year or two they all moved away, either to neighborhoods
where the Puerto Ricans and blacks weren't starting to move
in, or to Yonkers or Mount Vernon, and they started to have
babies and I'd visit them once or twice with gifts but it was
like we didn't have much in common anymore, and soon we
all lost touch.

And Vito and the Olinvilles kept turning out hits, even
though like I said, Vito never wrote another song after "Teenage Heartbreak." In addition to the doo-wop numbers, Vito had
begun letting loose on some slow, sexy ballads. I bought their
forty-fives and I bought their albums and every night after
work I would call up the radio stations and request their songs,
not that I needed to, since everyone else was requesting their
songs anyway, but it made me feel closer to Vito, I guess. And
sometimes I'd look at Vito's photograph on the album covers
or in the fan magazines and I'd see how his teeth and hair and
skin were perfect, there was no gap between his front teeth like
there used to be, no more acne, no more cowlick. And I kind of
missed those things, because that night when I gave myself to
Vito in the back seat of his older brother Danny's best friend
Freddy's car, I'd loved feeling Vito's rough, sandpapery skin
against mine and I'd loved letting my fingers play with his
cowlick and letting my tongue rest for a minute in the gap
between his front teeth.

So, for the next three, four years, I kind of lost count, Vito
and the Olinvilles ruled the airwaves. And every day I worked
at the Evander Sweet Store and every night I had dinner with
my parents and my mother would ask whether I was ever
going to get married and have babies and I'd say, "Come on,
Ma, leave me alone, I'm a good Catholic girl, of course I'm gonna have babies one day," and my father would say, "Geraldine,
if Pop ever tells me you're keeping late hours with any guys, I'll

kill you," and I'd say, "Come on, Pa, I told you, I'm a good Catholic girl," and then I'd help my mother with the dishes and then I'd kiss them goodnight and I'd go visit Pop for a few minutes in his apartment on the ground floor of the building and there would always be those strange men coming and going from his apartment and then I'd go upstairs to my own apartment and I'd sit in front of my mirror and I'd tease my hair up high and I'd put on my makeup and I'd put on my red prom dress and I'd listen to Vito's songs and I'd dance the lindy and the cha cha. And then before I went to sleep, I'd read through all the fan mags and I'd cut out every article about him and I'd paste them into my scrapbook.

Then one day, I don't remember exactly when, a couple of more years, maybe three, maybe even four, all I remember is that Carmela and Pamela and Victoria had all sent me announcements that they were on their second kids, the fan mags started printing fewer and fewer articles about Vito. I'd sit on my bed, thumbing through, and where before, I'd find at least one in every single mag, now I'd have to go through five, six, seven magazines and then I'd just find some real small mention of him. And the radio stations were playing Vito and the Olinvilles less and less often and I had to call in and request them more often because nobody else was doing it, and their songs weren't going higher than numbers fifteen or twenty on the charts. But Vito's voice was as strong and beautiful as ever, and the Olinvilles could still do those doo-wops in the background, so at first I felt really dumb, dumb, dumb because I couldn't figure out what was going on.

But I, Geraldine Rizzoli, am no fool, and it hit me soon enough. It was really simple. The girls my age were all mothers raising kids, and they didn't have time to buy records and dance the lindy and the cha cha in front of their mirrors. And the boys, they were out all day working and at night they sat and drank beer and watched football on TV. So a new generation of teenagers was buying records. And they were buying records by those British groups, the Beatles and the rest of them, and for those kids, I guess, an Italian boy from the Bronx with a pompadour wasn't very interesting. And even though I didn't look a day older than I had that night in the back seat of Vito's older brother Danny's best friend Freddy's car, and even though I could still fit perfectly into my red prom dress, I had to face facts, too. I wasn't a teenager anymore.

So more time went by, again I lost count, but Pop's hair was beginning to turn grey and my father was beginning to have a hard time lifting those crates of hot dogs and my mother seemed to be getting shorter day by day, and Vito and the Olinvilles never got played on the radio at all, period. And I felt bad for Vito, but mostly I was relieved, since I was sure then that he would come home. I bought new furniture, Pop put in new windows. I found a hairspray that made my hair stay higher even longer.

But I was wrong. Vito didn't come home. Instead, according to the few fan mags that ran the story, his manager tried to make him into a clean cut type, the type who appeals to the older Las Vegas set. And Vito left the Olinvilles, which, the fan mags said, was like Vito had put a knife through their hearts. One mag said that Vinny had even punched Vito out. Anyway, it was a mistake on Vito's part not to have just come home right then. He made two albums and he sang all these silly love songs from the twenties and thirties, and he sounded really off-key and miserable. After that, whenever I called the disk jockeys they just laughed at me and wouldn't even play his records. I'd have to go through ten or fifteen fan mags to find even a small mention of Vito at all. So I felt even worse for him, but I definitely figured he had to come home then. Where else could he go? So I bought a new rug and Pop painted the wall. And I sat in front of my mirror at night and I teased my hair and I applied my makeup and I put on my red prom dress and I danced the lindy and the cha cha and I played Vito's albums and I'd still cut out the small article here and there and place it in my scrapbook. And I hadn't aged a day. No lines, no wrinkles, no flab, no grey hair. Vito was going to be pleased when he came home.

But I was wrong again. Vito didn't come home. He went and got married to someone else, a skinny flat-chested blonde model from somewhere like Iowa or Idaho. A couple of the fan mags ran little pieces, and they said she was the best thing that had ever happened to Vito. Because of his love for her he wasn't depressed any more about not having any more number one hits. "Aay," he was quoted, "love is worth more than all of the gold records in the world." At first I cried. I kicked the walls. I tore some of the articles from my scrapbook and ripped them to shreds. I smashed some of his albums to pieces. I was really really angry, because I knew that it was me, Geraldine Rizzoli, who was the best thing that had ever happened to him! That blonde model had probably been a real goody-goody when she was growing up, the type who didn't cut classes or smoke or tease her hair or make out with lots of guys. No passion in her skinny bones, I figured. And then I calmed down. Because Vito would still be back. This model, whose name was Muffin Potts, was no threat at all. Vito would be back, a little ashamed of himself, but he'd be back.

Soon after that, Vito's mother and father died. A couple of fan mags carried the story. They died in a plane crash on their way to visit Vito and Muffin Potts in Iowa or Idaho or wherever she was from. I didn't get invited to the funeral, which was in Palm Beach. Vito's parents had moved there only six months after "Teenage Heartbreak" became number one. Five big moving vans had parked on Olinville Ave., and Vito's mother stood there in a fur coat telling everybody about the angel who'd visited her when she was pregnant with Vito. And I'd gone up to her and kissed her and said, "Good bye, Mrs. Venecio, I'm going to miss you," and she said, "Good bye, Carmela," like she was trying to pretend that she didn't remember that I was Geraldine Rizzoli, her future daughter-in-law. The fan mags had a picture of Vito at the funeral in a three piece suit, and the articles said he cried on the shoulder of his older brother Danny, who was now a distributor of automobile parts. There were also a couple of photos of Muffin Potts looking very bored.

Then I started to read little rumors, small items, in a few of the magazines. First, that Vito's marriage was on the rocks. No surprise to me there. I was surprised that it lasted an hour. Second, that Vito was heavy into drugs and that his addiction was breaking Muffin's heart. Really hard drugs, the mags said. The very worst stuff. One of the mags said it was because of his mother's death and they called him a "Mama's Boy." One said he was heartbroken because of his breakup with the Olinvilles and because Vinny had punched him out. And one said he'd been doing drugs ever since Evander Childs High School, and they had the nerve to call the school a "zoo," which I resented. But I knew a few things. One, Vito was no Mama's Boy. Two, Vito and the Olinvilles still all loved each other. And, three, Vito had never touched drugs in school. And if it were true that he was drowning his sorrows in drugs and breaking Muffin Pott's heart, it was because he missed me and regretted like hell not coming home earlier!

Soon after that I read that Muffin had left him for good and had taken their child with her. Child? I stared at the print. Ashley, the article said. Their child's name was Ashley. There was no photo, and since Ashley was a name with zero personality, I wasn't sure whether Ashley was a girl or boy. I decided it was a girl, and I figured she looked just like her mother, with pale skin and a snub nose and milky-colored hair, and I wasn't even slightly jealous of that child or her mother because they were just mistakes. True, Vito kept acting dumb, dumb, dumb, and making some big fat mistakes, but I didn't love him any less. A promise was a promise. And I, Geraldine Rizzoli, knew enough to forgive him. Because the truth was that even I had once made a mistake. The way it happened was this. One day out of the blue, who should come into the Evander Sweet Store to buy some cigarettes but Petey Cioffi, who'd been one of the guys in our crowd in the old days. A couple of years after graduation he married some girl from the Grand Concourse and we all lost touch. But here he was in the old neighborhood, visiting some cousins and he needed some cigarettes. Anyway, when he walked in, he stopped dead in his tracks. I could tell he was a little drunk, and he said, "Aay, Geraldine Rizzoli, I can't believe my eyes, you're still here, and you're gorgeous, I'm growing old and fat, look at this belly, but not you, you're like a Princess or something." And it was so good to be spoken to like that, and I let him come home with me. We made out in my elevator, and I felt like a kid again. I couldn't pretend he was Vito, but I could pretend it was the old days, when Vito was still chasing me and trying to get into my pants. In the morning, Petey said goodbye, looked at me one last time, shook his head and said, "Geraldine Rizzoli, what a blast from the past!" and he slipped out of the building before Pop woke up. He probably caught holy hell from his wife and I swear I got my first and only grey hair the next morning. But my night with Petey Cioffi made it easier to forgive Vito, since I'd made my mistake too. And I kept waiting. The neighborhood changed around me. The Italians left, and more and more Puerto Ricans and blacks moved in, but I didn't mind. Because everyone has to live somewhere, I figured, and I had more important things on my mind than being prejudiced.

    Then I pretty much stopped hearing about Vito altogether. And that was around when my father, bless his heart, had the heart attack on the hot dog truck and by the time they found him it was too late to save him, and my mother, bless her heart, followed soon after. I missed them so much, and every night I came home from work and I teased my hair at the mirror, I put on my makeup, I put on my red prom dress, I played Vito's songs, I danced the lindy and the cha cha, and I read through the fan mags looking for some mention of him, but there wasn't any. It was like he had vanished from the face of the earth. And then one day I came across a small item in the newspaper. It was about how Vito had just gotten arrested on Sunset Strip for possession of hard drugs, and how he was bailed out by Vinny of the Olinvilles, who was now a real estate salesman in Santa Monica. "I did it for old times sake," Vinny said, "for the crowd on Olinville Ave."

    The next morning, Pop called me to his apartment. He had the beginnings of cataracts by then and he hardly ever looked at the newspaper anymore, but of course, he'd spotted the article about Vito. His face was red. He was furious. He shouted, "Geraldine Rizzoli, you're like my own daughter, my own flesh and blood, and I never wanted to have to say this to you, but," he waved the newspaper ferociously, which was impressive, since his hands shook, and he weighed all of ninety pounds at this point, although he still dressed in his shiny black suits and those strange men still came and went from his apartment, "the time has come for you to forget Vito. If he was here I'd beat the living hell out of him." He flung the paper across the room and sat in his chair breathing heavily.

I waited a minute before I spoke just to make sure he was going to be okay. When his color returned to normal, I said, "Never, Pop. I promised Vito I'd wait."

"You should marry Ralphie."

"Ralphie?" I asked. Ralphie Pampino, who was part of the old crowd, too, had inherited the Evander Sweet Store from his father when Ralphie Sr. died the year before. It turns out that Ralphie Jr., who'd never married, was in love with me, and had been for years. Poor Ralphie. He'd been the kind of guy who never got to make out a whole lot. I'd always thought he looked at me so funny because he was constipated or had sinuses or something. But Pop told me that years ago Ralphie had poured out his heart to him. Although Pop had promised Ralphie that he'd never betray his confidence, the time had come. It seemed that Ralphie had his own spiritual mission: he was waiting for me. I was touched. Ralphie was such a sweet guy. I promised myself to start being nicer to him. I asked Pop to tell him about me and Vito, and I kissed Pop on the nose and I went back upstairs to my apartment and I sat in front of my mirror and I teased my hair and I put on my makeup and I put on my red prom dress and I listened to Vito's songs and I danced the lindy and the cha cha.

The next day, Ralphie came over to me and said, "Geraldine Rizzoli, I had no idea that you and Vito . . ." and he got all choked up and couldn't finish. Finally, he swallowed and said, "Aay, Geraldine, I'm on your side. I really am. Vito's coming back!" and he gave me the thumbs up sign and he and I did the lindy together right there in the Evander Sweet Store and we sang "Teenage Heartbreak" at the top of our lungs and we didn't care if any customers came in and saw us.

But after that there wasn't any more news about Vito, period. Most everyone on the block who'd known Vito and the Olinvilles was gone, and I just kept waiting. Just around that time an oldies radio station, WAAY, started up and it was pretty weird at first to think that Vito and the Olinvilles and all the other groups I had spent my life listening to were considered "oldies" and I'd look at myself in the mirror and I'd think, "Geraldine Rizzoli, you're nobody's oldie, you've got the same skin and figure you had the night that you gave yourself to Vito." But after awhile I got used to the idea of the oldies and I listened to WAAY as often as I could. I played it every morning first thing when I woke up and then Ralphie and I listened to it together at the Evander Sweet Store, even though most of the kids who came in were carrying those big radio boxes tuned to salsa or rap songs or punk and didn't seem to have any idea that there was already music on. Sometimes when nobody was in the store, Ralphie and I would just sing Vito's songs together. There was one DJ on the station, Goldie George, who was on from nine in the morning until noon and he was a real fan of Vito and the Olinvilles. The other DJs had their favorites too. Doo Wop Dick liked the Five Satins, Surfer Sammy liked the Beach Boys, but Goldie George said he'd grown up in the Bronx just two subway stops away from Olinville Ave. and that he and his friends had all felt as close to Vito as if they'd lived on Olinville Ave. themselves, even though they'd never met Vito or Vinny or Bobby or Richie. I liked Goldie George, and I wished he'd been brave enough to have taken the subway the two stops over so that he could have hung around with us. He might have been fun to make out with. One day Goldie George played thirty minutes straight of Vito and the Olinvilles, with no commercial interruptions, and then some listener called in and said "Aay, whatever happened to Vito anyway, Goldie George, he was some sort of junkie, right?"

"Yeah," Goldie George said, "but I'm Vito's biggest fan, like you all know, because I grew up only two subway stops away from Olinville Ave. and I used to feel like I was a close buddy of Vito's even though I never met him, and I happen to know that he's quit doing drugs and that he's found peace and happiness through the Chinese practice of Tai Chi and he helps run a mission in Bakersfield, California.

"Aay," the caller said, "Goldie George, you tell Vito for me that Bobby MacNamara from Woodside says, 'Aay, Vito, keep it up, man!'"

"I will," Goldie George said, "I will. I'll tell him about you, Bobby, because, being so close to Vito in my soul when I was growing up, I happen to know that Vito still cares about his loyal fans. In fact, I know that one of the things that helped Vito to get through the hard times was knowing how much his loyal fans cared. And, aay, Bobby, what's your favorite radio station?"

"WAAY!" Bobby shouted.

And then Goldie George played another uninterrupted thirty minutes of Vito and the Olinvilles. But I could hardly hear the music this time. I was sick to my stomach. What the hell was Vito doing in Bakersfield, California running a mission? I was glad he wasn't into drugs any more, but Bakersfield, California? A mission? And what the hell was Tai Chi? I was so pissed off. For the first time I wondered whether he'd forgotten my promise. I was ready to fly down to Bakersfield and tell him a thing or two, but I didn't. I went home, played my albums, danced, teased my hair, frowned at the one grey hair I'd gotten the night I was with Petey Cioffi, and I closed my eyes and leaned my head on my arms. Vito was coming back. He just wasn't ready yet.

About two weeks later I was behind the counter at the Evander Sweet Store and Ralphie was arranging some Chunkies into a pyramid when Goldie George said, "Guess what, everyone, all of us here at the station, but mostly Vito's biggest fan, me, Goldie George, have arranged for Vito to come back to his home town! This is Big Big Big Big News! I called him the other day and I said, Vito, I grew up two subway stops from you, and like you know, I'm your biggest fan, and you owe it to me and your other loyal fans from the Bronx and all the other boroughs to come back and visit and sing 'Teenage Heartbreak' for us one more time, and I swear Vito got choked up over the phone and he agreed to do it, even though he said that he usually doesn't sing any more because it interferes with his Tai Chi, but I said, Vito, we love you here at WAAY, man, and wait'll you hear this, we're going to book Carnegie Hall for you, Vito, not your grandmother's attic, but Carnegie Hall! How about that, everyone. And just so you all know, the Olinvilles are all doing their own things now, so it'll just be Vito alone, but hey, that's okay, that's great, Vito will sing the oldies and tickets go on sale next week!"

And I stood there frozen and Ralphie and I stared at each other across the counter, and I could see a look in his eyes that told me that he knew he'd finally lost me for good this time.

Because Vito was coming back. He may have told Goldie George that he was coming home to sing to his fans, but Ralphie and I both knew that it was really me, Geraldine Rizzoli, that he was finally ready to come back to. Vito worked in mysterious ways, and I figured that he finally felt free of the bad things, the drugs and that boring Muffin Potts and his own arrogance and excessive pride, and now he was pure enough to return to me. I wasn't wild about this Tai Chi stuff, whatever it was, but I could get used to it if it had helped Vito to get better so he could come home to me.

Ralphie sort of shook himself like he was coming out of some long sleep or trance. Then he came around the counter and put his arm around me in this brotherly way. "Geraldine Rizzoli," he said really softly, "my treat. A first row seat at Carnegie Hall."

But I wouldn't accept, even though it was such a beautiful thing for Ralphie to offer to do, considering how he'd felt about me all those years. I got teary-eyed. But I didn't need a ticket, not me, not Geraldine Rizzolli. Vito would find out where I lived and he'd come and pick me up and take me himself to Carnegie Hall. He'd probably come in a limo paid for by the station, I figured. Because the only way I was going to the concert was with Vito. I went home after work and I plucked the one grey hair from my scalp and then I teased my hair and I put on my makeup and I put on my red prom dress and I danced and sang.

All week Goldie George kept saying, "It's unbelievable, tickets were sold out within an hour! The calls don't stop coming, you all remember Vito, you all love him!"

On the night of the concert Pop came by. He had to use a walker to get around by then and he was nearly blind and lots of things were wrong. His liver, gall bladder, stomach, you name it. He weighed around seventy-five pounds. But he still out of his apartment. And he sat across from me on my sofa, beneath the velour painting of Jesus, and he said in a raspy voice, "Geraldine Rizzolli, I didn't ever want to have to say this, but you're like my own daughter, my own flesh and blood, and as long as Vito wasn't around, I figured, okay you can dance to his albums and tease your hair and wear the same clothes all the time and you're none the worse for it, but now that he's coming home I've got to tell you he won't be coming for you, Geraldine, if he cared a twit about you he would have flown you out to L.A. way back when and I'm sorry you let him into your pants and lost your cherry to him, but you're a middle-aged lady now and you're gonna get hurt real bad and I'm glad your mother and father, bless their souls, aren't around to see you suffer the way you're gonna suffer tonight, Geraldine, and I don't wanna see it either, what I want is for you to drive down to Maryland tonight real fast, right now, and marry Ralphie, before Vito breaks your heart so bad nothing will ever put it together again!"

I'd never seen Pop so riled up. I kissed him on the nose and I told him he was sweet, but that Vito was coming. And Pop left, shaking his head and walking slowly, moving the walker ahead of him, step by step, and after he left, I played my albums and I teased my hair and I applied my lipstick and I danced the lindy and the cha cha and I waited. I figured that everyone from the old crowd would be at the concert. They'd come in from the suburbs with their husbands and their wives and their children, and even, I had to face facts, in some cases, their grandchildren. And just then there was a knock on my door and I opened it and there he was. He'd put on some weight, but not much, and although he'd lost some hair he still had a pompadour and he was holding some flowers for me, and I noticed that they were red roses, which I knew he'd chosen to match my prom dress. And he said, "Aay, Geraldine Rizzoli, thanks for waiting." Then he looked at his watch. "All *right*, let's get a move on! Concert starts at nine." And I looked in the mirror one last time, sprayed on little more hairspray and that was it. Vito took my arm just the way he took it the night I gave myself to him in the back we went downtown by limo to Carnegie Hall, which was a real treat because I didn't get to go into Manhattan very often. And Carnegie Hall was packed, standing room only, and the crowd was yelling, "Aay, Vito! Aay, Vito! Aay, Vito!" and Pamela and Carmela and Victoria were there, and all the Olinvilles came and they hugged Vito and said there were no hard feelings, and Vinny and Vito even gave each other noogies on the tops of their heads, and everyone said, "Geraldine Rizzoli, you haven't aged a day." Then Goldie George introduced Vito, and Vito just got right up there on the stage and he belted out those songs, and at the end of the concert, for his finale, he sang "Teenage Heartbreak" and he called me up on stage with him and he held my hand and looked into my eyes while he sang. I even sang along on a few of the verses and I danced the lindy and the cha cha right there on stage in front of all those people. The crowd went wild, stamping their feet and shouting for more, and Goldie George was crying, and after the concert Vito and I went back by limo to Olinville Ave. and Vito gave the limo driver a big tip and the driver said, "Aay, Vito, welcome home," and then he drove away.

And ever since then Vito has been here with me in the two bedroom apartment. He still does Tai Chi, but it's really no big thing, an hour or two in the morning at most. Pop died last year and Vito and I were with him at the end and his last words were, "you two kids, you're like my own son and daughter." Vito works in the Evander Sweet Store now instead of me because I've got to stay home to take care of Vito Jr. and Little Pop, who have a terrific godfather in Ralphie and a great uncle in Vito's older brother, Danny. And, if I'm allowed to do a little bragging, which seems only fair after all this time, Vito Jr. and Little Pop are very good kids. They go to church on Sundays and they're doing real well in school because they never cut classes or smoke in the bathroom or curse, and Vito and I are as proud as we can be.

DAVIDA'S OWN

Davida found, nestled in the sand on the beach, something that resembled an earring, yet wasn't an earring, was, in fact, something superb. She was ten years old, on a summer vacation with her father and Linney, his lover.

Her father was a writer. She brought the shining object home for his examination; he noted his daughter's striking, immediate attachment and declared it, "An unknown metaphor!"

Linney was restless, wanting to go back to the city. "Come here, Pumpkin," she called to Davida, "let me see it—let's see what your father calls a 'metaphor.' "

Davida walked to where Linney sat in a lounge chair. "A metaphor?" Linney laughed. "For what? The Pollution Problem? It's just a rock."

Davida grabbed it back, looking to her father, hoping that he'd also be looking at her, since he had called it a metaphor—whatever that was—and Linney had merely declared it a rock, but he was too busy staring hard at Linney, with squinted eyes and a vertical line in his forehead, a look he'd often had on his face years ago when her mother still lived with them.

Davida saw her mother a few months every year. Her mother was an overweight woman who lived with her *own* mother, and Davida found the excess of weight, foods, and women all too much. If she were to reveal the metaphor during her next visit there, her mother would look at it for an instant, and then reach for something to eat, following that with a swig from her omnipresent bottle of diet soda.

Linney had appeared in Davida's life about six months before, young, thin, and nervous, which made Davida nervous, too. After about three days, Linney had begun calling Davida "Pumpkin" and asking which boys—and what they were like—Davida had crushes on. Davida had never had a "crush" in her whole life on *anyone*, and despite Linney's thin body, she reminded Davida of her mother and grandmother.

Davida's father had once had a novel published, and was in the process of trying to get another published, and still another written. He drank a little more than he should, chain-smoked low tar and nicotine cigarettes, sometimes called himself a "cliché" and occasionally looked at his daughter as if he wished she would just go away.

Davida was aware of all these people: her grandmother, her mother, her father the writer, and Linney, but she wasn't completely sure of what they were doing in her life. She knew that she was in the process of growing up in order to someday get *away* from her father and yet he was *everything*, and she suspected that Linney wasn't forever, while her mother and grandmother were both permanent and apart, like people from another planet.

What she had found on the beach, which at first she'd thought was an earring (she *loved* earrings, and hoped to be able to have her own ears pierced when she became a teenager, but she'd never wear the kind her mother wore, all red and blue fruits on gold-colored hoops) made a lot more sense to her than anything else that summer, including the beach itself. Her father insisted that she was to have fun swimming, making friends her own age with the children of other bored vacationers, building sand castles, exploring. Instead, she would find a solitary corner each morning (at home, or outside if she was told to) and stare at her treasure.

Davida's father's nickname for her was "Fish" because she was always thirsty. Food meant little to her (". . . a potential anorexia case?. . . " she'd once heard her father say when discussing, with a male friend of his over drinks, her disinterest in food, and the next day she'd made him explain, nodding seriously as he spoke, although really she found the whole idea dumb) but she loved to drink. Not Tab and Diet Dr. Pepper like her mother, not black coffee like Linney, not vodka martinis like her father—just water. Ice-cold tap water, or, when her father remembered to buy it, bubbling Perrier. Linney taught her how to slice lemon and squeeze it into the Perrier, and since Davida was always thirsty, there were bottles and jars filled with cold water in the refrigerator at all times. Sometimes her own thirst pained her: in the middle of the night she'd awaken three, four times with the urge to drink, and if she didn't obey, she couldn't sleep for the rest of the night.

The new treasure, however, cured her thirst, if she looked at it in a certain way, when the light was just right. Then her throat was calm, her stomach soothed.

The bathing suit her mother had given her that summer was a tangerine-colored bikini, really just two tangerine strips of elastic, one worn on top, one worn on botttom, so that she was able to stick the object into her belly button, between her tiny breasts, on the top of her sandy, tanned thighs, all of which felt wonderful, and although her throat might remain thirsty at those moments, other things felt better inside her when she lay on the sand, staring at the shining thing resting on her thigh, bordering the edge of her tangerine suit.

Linney went back to the city early, assuring Davida that *it had nothing to do with her*, that she loved Davida as if they were sisters or best girlfriends, but there were a few problems, she missed her job, her friends, also "your father has other needs," she'd added vaguely. Linney was driven into the city by Davida's father, who didn't return until late at night, leaving her all alone for the day. "I trust you," he'd said solemnly. "I'll bring you a gift." And he did: a book "for juveniles" about the practice of voodoo in Haiti, and that night, late as it was, he went through it with her, marveling at the drawings, explaining different things.

A few weeks later they also returned to the city, and then Linney began calling on the phone, and soon she was around just as much as before, although only for a few weeks, and then she was around less, and another woman, a chubby, short, red-haired woman named Pamela came over instead. It was obvious to Davida that for Pamela she didn't even exist, which, in a way, didn't bother her at all; one night she was in the kitchen at about eleven o'clock, drinking glass after glass of Deer Park spring water with lime (the supermarket, her father swore, had been out of both Perrier and lemons) when Pamela wandered in, wearing a sleeveless tank top shirt and nothing else, not even panties, and nudged Davida aside so she could reach for the strawberry ice-cream in the freezer. Davida handed two spoons to Pamela, who was obviously searching, not knowing in which drawer the silverware was kept. Pamela accepted the spoons without a word, and wandered sleepily back to the bedroom, closing the door behind her.

"Do you like Pamela?" her father asked one day soon after.

"Who?"

"You know who. Don't be cute. I'm too tired."

"No. She's voodoo."

He perked up, smiling suddenly; he was using magical symbolism in his new book. "Voodoo? Pamela? What do you mean?"

"Just that I'd like to put some curses on her, wipe her out with some spells!" Davida felt happy that she'd outsmarted her father at his own game.

He stopped smiling and lit up a cigarette. "Well, do you like Linney?"

Davida said nothing.

"Come on, baby, it's important to me. I want to know where *you're* coming from, and I want you to know where *I'm* coming from, okay?"

She squinted her eyes. "I'd rather not discuss any of this, Daddy," she said, and stood up. Her favorite object was in her room, beneath her pillow, and she wanted to go to it. Her father watched as she walked, almost ran, into her own room.

A week later it was announced that Davida would be spending two weeks with her mother and grandmother in their home, and that she would be allowed to pack her own suitcase for the first time. Linney called her on the phone to say goodbye, calling when her father was at his job at the agency ("my curse," he described it) so that Davida would know that this call was "only for her."

Davida's mother, heavier than ever, greeted her daughter in a maroon mu-mu, smelling strongly of flowery perfume. Her grandmother had fried an extravagant dinner of eggplant and noodles, and Davida broke out in hives—huge pink warts—an hour after dinner. "It must have been one of the spices," both women agreed, placing cold, wet handkerchiefs all over Davida's distorted skin.

After that, Davida caught the flu, and was chilled and heated for days, spending most of her visit beneath three heavy blankets in her mother's room.

When the fever broke, she was put into a taxi and sent back to her father's.

He kissed her and hugged her, and then sat her down. "Your mother was upset by that stone-thing you carry. She said that during your fever you talked to it, keeping it with you every second, and that even afterwards you refused to let them take it away from you. They said you carried it into the bathroom and to the dinner table. Is all that true?"

"Yes," said Davida, thinking, but I do all that here, too, what's the big deal all of a sudden?

For a minute her father said nothing. Then he put his hands on his thighs. "Well, I guess it's time we got rid of it then. I don't think it's healthy for anyone in my family to depend on external crutches. . . . I mean, we all do, to some extent, but that's too much of an extent, baby. . . ."

"It's a *metaphor*!" shouted Davida, certain that with that word, he'd take back the sick, awful things he was saying.

Her father lit up. "Metaphor? How do you know such a word? Tell me what that means, baby!"

She didn't answer.

"Tell me what you think it means, Davida, if you're using such a fancy word like that. You're calling your rock a metaphor, I want to know why!" Now he seemed angry.

"Because it is! Because . . ." she was wild, desperate, since everything, she knew, depended upon her answer. "It's not an earring, it's not a rock, it's *my own*!" She leaned back, frightened.

"Give it to me," her father demanded then, without hesitation. "Your mother said you were *obsessed*, and I refuse to see that happen to you this early. You've got all sorts of weird habits already, I think . . ." Now he was really speaking to himself, not to her. "The insomnia, the water, the talking aloud to yourself . . ."

"No," said Davida.

"Yes!" said her father, with the same look he'd had on his face right before her mother had left them once and for all.

She reached down into the pocket of her pink terry-cloth shorts, and handed him what was her own, her only own thing, not to be taken by any other living person, and now not hers any longer, just like that.

Her father's fist closed around it. He went into the bathroom, and she heard the flush. Then he came out. "Don't look so down," he said. "Metaphors crop up all the time, they really do."

Davida turned away, sorry to watch him being so silly. She'd be fine from here on in. She'd stop looking for magic and metaphors. If she was "obsessive" (and she knew the meaning of that term instinctively), then she'd turn completely the other way. She'd listen politely, without interest or curiosity, from corners, forever, getting her revenge on them all, growing into a stone-cold woman.

ROBIN'S NEST

Mr. Rosen, my social studies teacher, is standing in front of the blackboard and talking about the Vietnam War, which took place in the nineteen sixties. Mr. Rosen is my favorite teacher this year. For one thing, he has a red mustache, and I've loved red hair ever since I was a little girl. Robin, my mother, has red hair. But Mr. Rosen talks a lot, really fast, and Robin doesn't talk at all. Ever.

Mr. Rosen's hair isn't as beautiful as Robin's, though. Nobody has hair that beautiful. And I bet that if Robin could speak, her voice would be beautiful, too.

Ambrose, my boyfriend, also has red hair. Ambrose is in the sixth grade, like I am, but he goes to the Emerson School, which my dad says is too unstructured. I go to the Smythe-Durham School, which is very structured. I also like Mr. Rosen because he used to teach at the Emerson School, but I've never told my dad that. Right now, Mr. Rosen is saying that innocent people, even women and children, were killed during the war. I try to take notes while he speaks. But it's hard because I keep picturing the women and children, and they all start to look like me and Robin, and then I can't concentrate on his words. But I have to concentrate so that I can pass. I've been failing English since last year, and if I start to fail social studies too I don't know what my dad will do. It makes me nervous just thinking about it. So I start writing really fast, trying to copy down everything Mr. Rosen is saying. "President Johnson," I write down. "Amnesty for draft resisters," I write that down, too, but I'm not sure I know what amnesty means. Mr. Rosen must have said, but I guess I wasn't concentrating. Amnesty is a pretty word, though. I like the way it sounds. Maybe Ambrose and I can use it in Ooola, which is the private language he and I are inventing. Nobody in the whole world will know how to speak Ooola except me and Ambrose. But I can't think about Ooola now. I have to pay attention. Mr. Rosen is saying something about the draft resisters having to move to Canada. I know that my dad didn't like the draft resisters. My dad was an officer in the Marines in Vietnam, and he says that he lost close friends there, and that he and his friends were patriots, and that it was a good war. In Ooola, patriot means cappuccino. My dad says that the people who protested against the war were so self-indulgent and immature that they thought sex and rock 'n' roll were more important than freedom and honor. Or else they were crazy. He says that history will prove him right. Robin was a war protestor. Mr. Rosen is saying that he was a war protestor, too. "War protestor," I write down. I wonder if Robin and Mr. Rosen used to know each other during the nineteen sixties. Maybe Mr. Rosen even lived on Robin's commune with her.

Another thing I like about Mr. Rosen is that he talks about things I care about. For instance, last week he talked about the people in America who are so poor they have to live out on the streets, and how they get malnourished and freeze to death and other terrible stuff. He calls them "the homeless." I see

them, these homeless people, every day, when I walk through
the park on my way to and from Smythe-Durham. Sometimes
I even see homeless mothers with homeless children. I shiver
when I see them. My dad forbids me to give them dimes or
quarters or anything. He says it could be dangerous because
they're crazy. But I don't think most of them are crazy. And
even the ones who are deserve some dimes and quarters. But
Ambrose's father, who's a plastic surgeon like my dad, says
that it's good to give them dimes and quarters, so Ambrose
gives for both of us. Robin never carries money, but one day
last winter, she and I were walking in the park and we passed a homeless woman who was only half dressed. Robin was
wearing a big baggy black coat. She took it off and gave it to
the woman. I bet my dad wouldn't have liked that if he'd been
with us.

The bell rings. I close my notebook. Mr. Rosen says that
the only homework we have tonight is to think about whether it's okay to disagree with your government. Or with your
parents. He smiles. He has a nice smile.

Next I have my session with Ms. Ullman, the psychologist
at Smythe-Durham. Last year when I started failing English,
the headmaster, Dr. Prescott, who has almost no hair at all,
called me into his office, which was filled with ships in bottles. He said, "Your reading scores are extremely high, young
lady. You shouldn't be failing English." I didn't say anything.
So he said that he was going to send me to see Ms. Ullman.
He said my dad had called him and was very unhappy that
I wasn't passing English. And he said he didn't want my dad
to be unhappy.

I knock on Ms. Ullman's door and she says, "Come in,
Rachel." Ms. Ullman's office is nice, much nicer than Dr.
Prescott's office, and I like sitting in the big brown leather
chair across from her. Above her desk there's a painting of
a big red bird sitting on the branch of a tree. I once asked
Ms. Ullman if the bird was a robin, and she said she didn't
think so. She said it was more like a bird painted from the
artist's imagination. I like to look up at the red bird when we
talk because that bird's eyes are big and sad, like Robin's.

Ms. Ullman and I talk a lot about birds, because when I was little I used to think that Robin wasn't really my mother, but that she was some strange bird that had flown into our apartment. I figured that she had a broken wing and couldn't fly home. Sometimes I thought that she was a lost bird from another planet.

The thing is, Robin really does look more like a bird than a mother. At least, she doesn't look like the mothers of the other kids I know. And she doesn't act like them, either. Ambrose's mother, for example, is tall and she wears high heeled shoes which make her look taller and blouses with padded shoulders and she talks all the time. But Robin is very small, and she wears simple dresses that just slip over her head, and flat sandals. And she's always looking over her shoulder, like birds do. And she has those big sad bird eyes. Even sadder than the eyes of the red bird on Ms. Ullman's wall. And she has long hair that goes way past her waist, so that sometimes it looks like bright red feathers are growing down her back. Ms. Ullman thinks it's good that I've accepted that Robin really is my mother, and not a bird.

Ms. Ullman and I also talk a lot about my dad. My dad does nose jobs and face lifts and tummy tucks and breast enlargements. Sometimes he calls himself a "sculptor." He also calls himself "Pygmalion," which Ambrose says is the title of a play about a rich man who wants to make a poor woman act rich. Most of my dad's patients are women. They come from all over the world, he says, "because I speak their language, Rachel. They all want to be beautiful, and I speak the language of beauty." Sometimes he tells me and Robin stories about his patients, like the woman who had a nose like Jimmy Durante's, but wanted a nose like Marilyn Monroe's, or the woman who was flat-chested and had never had a boyfriend but after my dad gave her bigger breasts she had two boyfriends. "I gave her perfect breasts," he said, looking right at Robin who has really tiny breasts, almost no breasts at all, and what she has she hides completely underneath baggy dresses. Robin looks over her shoulder when he says things like that. But I say, "Really, Daddy?" and "Wow, Daddy," because I'm too scared not to act excited about his work. I'm scared that when I grow up he's going to want to do those jobs on me, too. Ambrose says I shouldn't be scared, that he won't let him. But I don't know. I'm afraid that if I don't grow up to be beautiful enough, he'll start sculpting me.

Since Ms. Ullman encourages me to talk to her about my fears, I've told her that lately I've noticed that my nose is starting to grow. "It's not a tiny pug nose any more like it was when I was little, and I'm afraid my dad will notice it soon," I say.

"You have a lovely nose, Rachel," Ms. Ullman says. "Honestly."

I don't ever want my dad to meet Ms. Ullman. I'm afraid he'll want to do something to her nose, too. Ms. Ullman has short frizzy brown hair, but sometimes, when the sun shines through her office window, her hair looks almost red. And she has big thick eyebrows and a long hooked nose with a bump on it. Ambrose met her one Saturday morning when he and I were sitting on a bench in the park, practicing Ooola and counting out change to give to homeless people. Ms. Ullman walked by. She looked different in blue jeans and a sweatshirt. She came over and said, "How nice, that you both care so much about the less fortunate." "She's intense looking," Ambrose said after she left. But I don't think my dad would find intense beautiful.

The very first thing Ms. Ullman ever said to me during our very first session was, "So I hear you're having some trouble in your English class." But I just shrugged. I didn't want to talk about English class. I looked up at the painting of the red bird. "Is it okay if we forget the English class stuff today?" I asked. "Can I tell you something else instead?"

She didn't answer right away. And then she gave me a big smile and said, "Shoot!" So I took a deep breath, and I told her the story of how my dad met Robin and why Robin doesn't ever speak. I told it exactly the way my dad tells it to me. "Robin was in a hospital because she'd taken all this LSD during the nineteen sixties and it had made her stop speaking," I said. Ms. Ullman began taking notes. "My dad says that LSD is a drug that makes you see the world as though you're crazy. It ruins your mind like a . . ." But I had to stop there because my dad always says, "like a bump and a hook ruin a nose," and I didn't want to repeat that in front of Ms. Ullman. So I just said, "Anyway, Robin had taken a lot of it. My dad was working in the hospital. He says that from the first moment he saw her, sitting on top of her bed in her hospital gown, staring over her shoulder, he knew what he wanted. 'I wanted to take her home, Rachel,' he says. 'To heal her, to make her whole again. I saw that there was something special about her. Her suffering had enriched her. It was my duty. I would be a plastic surgeon of the mind. Instead of a nose job, I would give your mother a mind job.'"

Ms. Ullman looked up from her notes. "A mind job?" she asked. "Those are your father's words?"

I nodded.

"Did he . . . smile when he said it?" she asked.

I shrugged. "I can't remember."

"Well . . . just what is a . . . mind job?"

"I'm not sure," I said. "I think he . . . talked to her a lot. About the things he wanted her to believe in. Things that would make her less crazy. Things for her. . . own good."

Ms. Ullman took a wrinkled handkerchief from her desk and blew her nose.

"Anyway, he took her home and married her. And he gave her the mind job. And then they had me." I didn't say anything else because I wasn't sure what else to say. That's where my dad always stops when he tells the story.

"A mind job," Ms. Ullman said again. She was writing really fast now.

"I'm afraid," I said.

"Afraid, Rachel?" Ms. Ullman put down her pen and leaned forward and looked into my eyes. "What are you afraid of?"

"I'm afraid that a mind job hurts."

"Oh," she said. "Well, has Robin . . . gotten better?"

"My dad says yes," I said. "He says that even though she doesn't speak she's not crazy or unhappy anymore and that she believes in all the right things and that she would never do the kinds of things she used to do like protest against the Vietnam War and take drugs and live in a commune and dance naked at hippie festivals and not buy from the military-industrial complex and not give money to taxes because the money is spent on weapons and things like that. . . ."

"And what do you think?"

"I don't know." And then I told her that when I used to think Robin was a bird from another planet I also believed that she was really speaking all the time, but that people on earth just couldn't hear her because her language was on a higher frequency than earth ears could hear. "Even though she doesn't say so, I know Robin loves me," I explained to Ms. Ullman. I told her that Robin takes me on long walks through the park and that when I have a fever she sits by my bedside for hours and holds my hand and puts wet towels on my forehead, and that she sometimes sits with me and Ambrose and we all eat tuna fish sandwiches together. Ms. Ullman said that Robin sounded like a very caring person, and I felt happy when she said that.

Sometimes Ms. Ullman doesn't say anything at the beginning of the session. She just lets me start talking about anything I want to. But other times she starts by asking me a question, and today the first thing she asks me to do is describe our apartment. "I'd like to have a sense of your home," she says. "Tell me about it, Rachel."

"It's very big," I tell her. "My dad has a bedroom and a study, and Robin and I each have a bedroom, and there's a living room and a kitchen and a dining room. And last year my dad put this white furniture all over the place. It's kind of like a hospital now, and he doesn't like it if there's the slightest bit of dirt on anything."

Ms. Ullman waits for me to say something else. But I don't have anything else to say about the white furniture.

"Any other thoughts about your home?" Ms. Ullman runs her hand through her frizzy hair.

So I tell her about how one day I told my dad that I felt guilty about how big our apartment was, because there are so many homeless people. I said maybe we had more than our fair share of space. He said that I shouldn't feel guilty, that most of the homeless people wouldn't know how to survive in an apartment building like ours anyway, that they wouldn't want the responsibilities of mortgages and coop board meetings and things like that, and that chopping a bedroom or two off of our apartment wouldn't solve the homeless problem. Ms. Ullman asks, "Did he smile when he said those things?" But I shrug. "I can't remember."

Then Ms. Ullman says, "You're a very caring girl, Rachel."

I'm glad that Ms. Ullman thinks I'm a caring girl. I also hope she thinks I'm pretty just the way I am. Sometimes my dad takes my face in his hands and looks at it from different angles and I get very scared.

"So," Ms. Ullman says, leaning back, "how's Ooola going?" Ms. Ullman asks me about Ooola a lot during our sessions. After I'd had a few sessions with her, I told her about it because I knew I could trust her. I told her that sometimes Ambrose and I invent brand new words to mean things, words which sound like nonsense to anyone else. And that other times we take words that already mean something in English but we make them mean something else, which is just as good as inventing a new word, and that we're going to have a whole Ooola dictionary some day which only we'll know how to read. And a grammar handbook, too.

"Ambrose found the word ablutions in the dictionary yesterday," I tell her. "It means a ceremonial washing of oneself." Ms. Ullman may know this already, but I can't be sure. "But in Ooola, it's going to mean sad." Sometimes I tell Ms. Ullman a few words in Ooola. Ambrose says it's okay, because even if I tell her a few words, she still won't know enough to speak it. "Today after school Ambrose and I are going to invent words for colors," I tell her. "Last week we invented words for the seasons. Cratoup means winter."

"Cratoup," she repeats, blowing her nose.

She puts away her handkerchief and looks serious for a minute. "Maybe, Rachel," she says softly, "the reason you're inventing Ooola has something to do with the reason you're not passing English. What do you think of that idea?"

I don't say anything. Ms. Ullman comes up with weird ideas like this all the time.

"Well, I'm afraid that our time is up for today," Ms. Ullman says, looking at her watch.

"Arugula, " I say to her, which is Ooola for goodbye.

"Arugula," she says.

My next class is English. I dread it. This year I was put in a slow class, even though Dr. Prescott said my reading scores are so high. It's a punishment for failing, I guess. Ms. Buschel is my English teacher. She's got blonde hair and a tiny nose. She's the type, I think, that my dad has in mind when he fixes noses. I always sit in the back of the room, hoping that she won't remember I'm there. Today she tells us to write, stories about anything we want. I wish I could write my story in Ooola. But if I did that I'd be afraid Ms. Buschel would show it to Dr. Prescott and then they'd send me to a hospital like Robin was in. And then my dad would definitely want to do a mind job on me. I force myself to pick up my pen and write.

Ms. Buschel says, "Okay, that's enough writing time. Now we'll call on a few of you to share your stories. How about Carl first?" Carl walks to the front of the room. He licks his lips. His story is about a little boy who wants a donkey for Christmas more than anything else in the world, and then on Christmas morning Santa Claus gives him one. Everyone applauds. Ms. Buschel says, "Okay, everyone, let's give Carl some feedback." Annie raises her hand and says, "It made me feel good that he got the donkey." "Very perceptive, Annie. And thank you, Carl, for sharing your story," Ms. Buschel smiles.

I pray that Ms. Buschel doesn't call on me next. "Nancy," she says. Nancy walks to the front of the room. She holds the paper right in front of her face while she reads. Her story is about a little girl who wins a pie baking contest and starts a pie business and becomes a millionaire. Everyone applauds. Ms. Buschel asks for feedback. "It's good because she succeeds," Nicky says. "Very insightful, Nicky. And thank you, Nancy, for sharing that," Ms. Buschel says.

I pray again that Ms. Bushel doesn't call on me. But this time I'm not so lucky. "Rachel," she says. I walk to the front of the room. I clear my throat and read. "There was a little girl whose mother was a beautiful silent bird from another planet. The little girl's father said the little girl's mother was crazy. So he gave her mother something he called a mind job. But a mind job hurts. It pushes words down into your brain. So the little girl started to speak a special, secret language that nobody else would understand. That way nobody could ever give her a mind job." Nobody applauds. Nobody gives feedback. Ms. Buschel doesn't thank me for sharing my story. So I sit down and some other students get up and read their stories, but I don't pay any attention. Instead, I think about what amnesty could mean in Ooola and about Ambrose and Robin and the red bird on Ms. Ullman's wall.

English is the last class of the day, and when the bell rings, I race out. Ambrose is waiting for me on the corner. "Mubbles," I say to him, which means hello in Ooola. "Mubbles, Rachel," he says.

I met Ambrose last year when my dad was giving a speech about a new technique in nose jobs. It was a whole afternoon of plastic surgeons speaking about cutting and pulling and bending. I went because it seemed like a way for me to act really interested in my dad's work. I was sitting by myself in the front row. I was the only kid in the whole auditorium. But then Ambrose came in. He sat down right next to me. He pointed towards the doctors sitting on stage waiting for their turns to speak. "That one's mine," he pointed to a roly-poly, red-headed man on the left side of the stage. "Which one's yours?"

Ambrose's father is really different than my dad. His father mostly works on people who've been burned in fires or injured in accidents. He tries to make them look the way they looked before they got hurt.

I fell in love with Ambrose the instant he sat down next to me. He says that he fell in love with me right then too. He says that unconsciously we'd already begun communicating with each other in Ooola. I was nervous about what Ambrose would say the first time I brought him home and introduced him to Robin, but he didn't blink an eye. He's very sensitive. He writes love poems to me in both English and Ooola. He's even asthmatic, which makes me love him more. Because I know he needs taking care of.

Ambrose takes my hand as we walk across the park. The Smythe-Durham School is on the east side of the park, and I live on the west side. I'm glad because that way we get to walk through the park every day and Ambrose can give quarters and dimes to the homeless people who live in the grass and trees. Sometimes he drops the money into their cups, sometimes right into the palms of their hands. Some of them say "God bless you." Some of them say, "Hey, Carrot Top." And some of them don't say anything. I wonder if the ones who don't say anything are really speaking to us in a language on another frequency.

When we get to my building, the doorman, Billy, who likes Ambrose, gives him a special handshake. "It's from the nineteen sixties," Billy says. "It's called a power-to-the-people shake." Ambrose and I give power-to-the-people shakes to each other in the elevator on the way upstairs. I wonder if Robin used to shake hands like that before she took too much LSD. In the elevator, Ambrose also gives me a little kiss right on the tip of my nose, which I'm sure he does because I told him that it's growing. "Swampy," I say to him, which means thank you in Ooola.

We walk inside the apartment. The first thing I always do is look around for Robin. When I was little I used to look around because I was worried that she'd flown away while I was gone, but now I do it just because I like to. But I don't see her, so I figure she's in her bedroom. Ambrose and I go into the kitchen and make tuna fish sandwiches. I like mine with more onions than he does and he likes his with more mayonnaise. What we both like is to make them thick, with lots of lettuce and tomatoes crammed in. And we both like them on hard rolls with seeds. My dad disapproves of the way I eat. He tells me I'm not too young to start counting calories. But since he won't be home until much later, I stuff my sandwich to the limit.

Then Ambrose and I pour ourselves some cherry seltzer, which is my favorite flavor, and we go into the living room and get ready to work on inventing words for colors. We sit on the rug, and we surround ourselves with all of my dad's dictionaries and thesauruses. We even take his medical dictionaries out and use words from them. For instance, in Ooola, Cortisone means dinnertime, and Tetracycline means helicopter. We have to be very careful not to get tuna fish on the white rug.

Robin wanders in. I'm happy to see her. I smile at her. She's wearing a baggy light blue dress. She takes tiny bird steps. She smiles back at us and wanders past us into the kitchen.

Ambrose says, "How about sponge for blue?"

I try it out. "Robin is dressed in sponge today."

"Now I'm not sure," Ambrose says. "Did that sound right to you?"

"Well, let's think about the meaning of blue." That's how we work. We think about what words mean to us. I once explained our method to Ms. Ullman and she told me that what we do is called free associating.

I begin. "The sky."

"The sea," Ambrose says.

I say, "My dad says that women with blue eyes get the most upset if their noses are big because they feel gypped, like since they got the blue eyes they should have also gotten the tiny noses."

"Bluefish," Ambrose says.

"My dad says that the blue in the black and blue marks that women get on their skin after face lifts is a unique shade of blue, not found anywhere else."

"Singin' the blues," Ambrose says.

Robin comes in from the kitchen and sits down with us. She tucks her legs under her dress. She's made herself a tuna fish sandwich too. She hardly uses any mayonnaise or onions at all, and her sandwich is much thinner than ours. Ambrose and I take big bites of our sandwiches. Robin takes tiny bird-sized bites. I want to say something to her but I don't know what to say. When I was little I used to say things like, "Pretty bird, fly." But now I'm usually just quiet around her. What I want to say most of all is that I hope it didn't hurt too much when my dad gave her the mind job. I believe that my dad wouldn't hurt her deliberately. I believe that he loves her too. But he has this saying that he uses a lot, "The end justifies the means." Ms. Ullman says if I want to ask Robin about the mind job, maybe I should just come out and ask.

"Listen," I say to Ambrose instead, "I think I like sponge for blue."

Ambrose smiles. He has these wonderful crooked teeth that braces just don't seem to help. "I get the sponges most every night," he says.

Robin takes a sip from my glass of cherry seltzer. And then she clears her throat. It's a tiny sound. Ambrose and I both stare at her. I've never heard any noise come from her throat before. Robin turns away from us and looks over her shoulder. Then she turns back and takes another sip of seltzer. She clears her throat again. Ambrose takes my hand. I hold onto his hand for dear life. We keep staring at her.

"Children," Robin says.

I hear it clearly. It's the first word Robin has ever spoken to me. Her voice is soft and sad. It's the voice that birds really would speak in if they could, I'm sure.

"Children," Robin says again.

I can't say a word. I look at Ambrose. He's having trouble breathing. I'm afraid he's going to have an asthma attack and I won't be able to take care of him because I'm in a state of shock. But luckily Ambrose calms down. He takes deep breaths and counts to ten. He begins breathing normally again and color returns to his face. And he actually answers her, like he's just having a regular conversation with anyone. "Uh huh?" he asks.

Robin looks over her shoulder and then back at us. I'm sure she won't answer. Maybe someone put LSD into our tuna fish sandwiches and Robin never spoke at all. Maybe we just imagined her voice. But I'm wrong. She answers. She speaks very slowly. She stops between words. She looks as though she's concentrating and working very hard on speaking. "Children. I know that . . . you are inventing . . . new words. . . . A new . . . language."

"Mother," I say, finally, putting down my sandwich, "Why haven't you spoken all these years?" My hand in Ambrose's is all sweaty. I feel like a very very little girl, much younger than eleven. I also feel like an old woman, maybe a hundred years old. I can't believe that I'm asking her this and that she's going to answer me.

Robin waits a minute before speaking. This time her words come more quickly. She's not stumbling so much. "I chose not to speak. It was my own choice. I'd grown very sad. But now . . . I speak because I'm so very pleased . . . that you care so much, Rachel . . . the way I did."

I don't say anything for a minute. I feel so surprised. All these years Robin could have talked, but she didn't want to because she was sad. I remember a word my dad used once. "Disillusioned," he said. "Your mother, Rachel, had grown disillusioned." I keep staring at Robin and I start to feel very sad, myself. I don't like the sound of the word disillusioned. I don't want to include it in Ooola.

Ambrose squeezes my hand and says, "It's spaghetti." Spaghetti means okay in Ooola. I squeeze his hand back. And then I take Robin's hand and I squeeze it, too. She squeezes back. She holds my hand tight.

And I think that maybe Ambrose and I don't need to keep Ooola a secret from everyone. Maybe it would be wonderful if one day everyone in the whole world spoke only Ooola. And there wouldn't be any words in Ooola for homelessness or crime or prisons or wars or mind jobs and nobody would want a different skin color or a smaller nose or larger breasts. Everyone would feel fine just the way they were. And Robin would talk all the time, because she wouldn't be disillusioned, and my dad would only do plastic surgery on people who'd been injured. Even though Robin didn't know about Ooola during the nineteen sixties, I guess that was the way she wanted it too. But she failed. At least, she thought she failed. But maybe what she's saying now is that, because of me, she hasn't really failed.

I feel shy and I look at Ambrose. Ambrose says, "It's spaghetti."

THE DREADED FEMALE
LOCKER ROOM TALK

U nabashedly, almost obsessively, we stare at each other's bodies in the locker room, and we talk and talk
and talk.

Since I've lived in five cities in the last six years, I know
that this isn't a phenomenon unique to one particular locker
room in one particular gym in one particular city. In each city,
I've joined something: a Y, an adult education swim class, an
outrageously expensive health club, an aerobics group in a
church basement. . . .

During the periods when I'm packing to move and arranging mail-forwarding and making farewells, I don't get a
chance to go to the gym very often. My moves usually follow

an exhausting period of grading final exams all night long, which usually follows an exhausting period of job hunting, during which I do little else but scan professional journals and compose job letters and travel to conferences, all of which preclude breaks for swimming or running or Nautilus, or even ten minutes on an exercise bike.

Finally I land a new one-year position and I move. I put up bookshelves and hang prints in my new apartment and begin writing letters to friends, congratulating the lucky ones who got tenure and commiserating with the ones who didn't.

September and October fly by with preparation for classes and faculty meetings and dinner invitations and then around November I step on a scale or I drive to the local mall and try on a pair of slacks. The next day, I speak to the women faculty and to the department secretaries. There is always at least one aerobic dance class. Somewhere. Always.

In graduate school, a joke sprang up among the female students whenever we spotted a group of male students together. "Look," we'd giggle, "they're at it again—they're talking that dreaded male locker room talk again. . . ."

I was dating Pat Wooster, whose dissertation was going to be a comparison of metaphors in Pound and Conrad. He had been a jock in his high school somewhere in West Virginia. "Tell me," I said once, when I was a little tipsy, "all about the dreaded male locker room talk. I mean, what's it all about—really?"

He looked at me and laughed. "Jesus, Gold," he said—he always called me by my last name, a trait I'd found initially endearing, but which, by the time we broke up in March, I detested—"I'd never reveal that to . . . a girl!"

Only after I'd moved to a small city down South for my first job did I realize that I no longer looked quite as firm as the blonde sophomores in their blue jeans and tank-tops. So I learned to huff and puff and I learned that it's fine to sweat, and that it's fine to look at women without their clothes on and to be looked at by them, but most important, I learned that there is female locker room talk, too, which doesn't have to do with advice about mascara and lipstick and perfume, although that might be part of it. Nor about recipes for banana bread and stir-fried vegetables in ginger sauce, although that might be part of it, too. Nor exclusively about the latest in painless bulimia. Nor how to snare a man, nor how to tell if your man is cheating, nor how to cheat on your man successfully, nor how to perform exotic tricks in bed, nor how to find God, nor how long to safely remain in the sauna, nor how to lift weights without growing bulky, nor managerial-level job openings in the local department store, nor how to choose the perfect running shoe, nor how to confront your boss without crying, nor therapists and their rates, nor breast feeding, nor mortgages, nor crime in the streets, nor how to keep spider plants from turning brown at the edges, nor non-sexist books for children, nor the first signs of Alzheimer's Disease, nor how to check for lumps in your breasts, nor whether there will ever be a socialist government in America, nor whether Vitamin B taken before you go to sleep really prevents hangovers, nor whether love lasts and hatred never expressed turns inward and causes cancer.

And we towel ourselves off and blow our hair dry, unabashedly staring at each other and noting our flabbiness, our firmness, our stretch marks, our beauty . . . noting who shaves where and who doesn't, who pushes the scale back to zero and who leaves it proudly at her weight, who preens naked before the full-length mirror and who hides and ducks her head. And all the while we keep talking that dreaded female locker room talk.

It's April now, and I know that soon I'll have to be moving on again. Somewhere, a position will open up for me, and I'll replace someone who'll be on sabbatical no longer than three semesters. This means new classes to prepare for, a new apartment to decorate, a new city to find my way around in, and, naturally, a new locker room.

SAFE

Michael leaned across the table in the Italian restaurant and placed his finger lightly on Marissa's wrist to steady it as she poured some red wine into their slender-stemmed wine glasses. Marissa embarrassed herself by the way she reacted to his touch, she felt strong desire, the kind those tacky paperback books she used to read before she went to college called a "burning desire" and it was unbelievable to her, that just the touch of a man's fingers on her wrist could make her feel this way, when in her entire life she'd never felt this way before. She could swear she was shivering and turning red, and she felt hot and cold and out of breath all at the same time. She'd been so tame . . . so sheltered, really, so sweet, so overprotected by her parents, by the affluent suburb she grew up in. She'd been the kind of nice girl who never went anywhere without her mother's permission, and she feared sex as she'd been taught to, feared boys who might be out to use her. Her mother was more old-fashioned than some of the other girls' mothers in Woodmere, but even the mothers who hadn't minded that their daughters had sex with their boyfriends didn't want their daughters to love it and crave it, they just wanted their daughters to become versed in it so that one day when they got married to some rich safe man they'd be able to do what was required of them. She had been the kind of girl who listened to her mother's views on love and marriage and family, and the most she let her high school boyfriend, Buddy, do was kiss her on the lips and she didn't even exactly kiss back, just sort of puckered and tried to breathe a little heavy. There had been almost no feeling between her and Buddy, she knew it even then, they never spoke of deep things, never spoke at all, really, he just hung around with her crowd, the good kids with good grades, and Buddy wasn't the best looking or the brightest in the crowd so she wasn't intimidated by him, she didn't have to test herself in any way, it had all been so safe, approved by all the parents in Woodmere, most of whom were one another's best friends, too. In college she chose her boyfriend because she liked him, which was a big step forward. Harry was a philosophy major and what she liked best was his animation about obscure things, she liked going to foreign films with him so he could explain the symbolism to her afterwards, and being with Harry was a slight rebellion against her parents and her upbringing because his excitement about obscurities and abstractions probably wouldn't translate into good business sense, into dollars and cents, and yet when she and Harry kissed she didn't feel much more than she had with Buddy, although they did go all the way, finally, in her junior year, and she'd lain in Harry's arms, thinking, no, this can't be all, there must be more, like in all those foreign films he took her to, and in the books she'd been reading in her classes, for she too had fallen in love with obscurity and abstraction, and had become a comparative lit major. Harry and she broke up senior year, they just drifted apart, one day she saw him at the movies explaining the symbolism to another girl, and years later she heard that he'd married that girl and was teaching philosophy at a small college down south. She moved to Manhattan after graduation, her father knew someone at a real estate firm in SoHo and she convinced the boss that her intellectual skills would be invaluable in the cutthroat real estate world, and she moved up the ladder, was making very good money, but she continued to read books, not just what was on the best-seller lists, she read slim, esoteric volumes of poetry and she went to foreign films and the opera and the ballet and she was always drawn to romantic themes, to love and passion. But she was in her mid-twenties and she'd never felt deeply for a man, in fact, she felt more deeply for her cats, Hester and Tess, and she had never lusted, never really been lusted after, except by weird men on the subways, and they didn't count. But at least, looking on the bright side, with what was going on these days she was certain that she was safe. Yes, her lack of desire for the men around her had kept her pretty darned safe, she could be sure of that. If she'd been the lusty, promiscuous type, on the other hand, she might not be safe, not that women were supposed to be at high risk, anyway, but you never knew. All those women's magazines warning women to abstain, or only to be with men who'd been tested, well, not that a test would prove they were absolutely safe, the article would add, nothing could prove it, ever . . . so that was the bright side about having been with one dull man years ago. There had been two men she'd dated since college, someone at work, and the son of a friend of her father's, but she'd dated them only a few times each and then couldn't imagine marrying them and bearing their children, let alone going to bed with them, and the dates had stopped. So there was the bright side, safety in lack of numbers. But she'd been so bored, and didn't being bored put you at risk too? At risk of losing your zest for life, your energy, of becoming old before your time? Wasn't that a kind of death, too? All along her life had been so safe, too safe. Not that safe had been associated with life versus death until recently, safe had merely meant a nice, ordinary house in the suburbs, money in the bank, two or three vacations a year, everything she'd been brought up to believe in. The American Dream. Which she wanted very much. And didn't want at all. The idea of living a safe little life in the suburbs, knowing only people exactly like herself, with her skin color and her religious leanings and her values, in houses made out of "ticky tacky" like the words in the old folk song she'd once heard, was terrifying. But was it as terrifying as dying? She had no way of knowing. On the other hand, she wanted, like most women, she was sure, the other side of the American Dream, which she'd been promised too, which was that in the beginning, before the house in the suburbs, love was not bland and bells would ring and lights would go off when she and her true love kissed for the first time. She wanted unbearable tension, a man who would kiss her neck for hours, who would take each of her fingers and kiss them one by one, a man who knew how to touch and stroke, who understood about romance, who wasn't embarrassed by passion, who didn't think passion was wimpy, who would know where to touch her, and how, and when. And now she'd found that man. She intuited it, she knew it. That man was Michael, whom she'd met through her job. He was apartment hunting. He was her age and a singer in a band that played the downtown club scene, and he worked at the deli across the street from her office during the day to support himself and he'd come in this morning and sat at her desk and they'd talked about rentals versus coops, and luckily his parents were willing to help him out because otherwise she wouldn't have had a single thing in his price range, and then he left and she happened to go to the deli at lunchtime and they talked some more and then she worked past six and found herself at the deli just when he was getting off and they walked to this restaurant together and it wasn't a date, it had happened casually, naturally, she wasn't even sure which of them had suggested that they continue their conversation over dinner . . . but she knew, she sensed, that Michael was sensual and experienced and unashamed, everything Buddy and Harry weren't, and that he felt something strong for her, that she had touched something off in him, and he in her, and that he would not find her body alien and intimidating, he would identify with her, empathize with her. But was Michael safe? She doubted it, for some reason, she sensed it in the same way she sensed his passion, and it made her so sad. And there was no way to be sure, a test wasn't enough, and anyway, she couldn't just come out and say, oh by the way have you been tested and how recently? He was so beautiful, so amazingly beautiful, she'd spotted him the second he'd come into the office even before he'd come to her desk, the instant he walked through the door, she thought, *what a beauty*, which wasn't something she ever thought about men, it was a way of thinking that was foreign to her, but he was a different species than Buddy and Harry, with his thick blonde hair and his full mouth, which was a bit pouty, very masculine and at the same time almost flowery, like a European film star. When he sat at her desk, she felt aware of herself as a sexual being in a way that she never did at work, not that certain kinds of men didn't try to put the moves on her, but those men were such boors, and she never responded to their flirtatiousness. With Michael, though, she'd crossed her legs and been aware of the rustling sound of her pantyhose and when she leaned forward to show him a brochure about a new building going up on the West Side, she could barely remember what she was showing him, because she became too aware that the conservative silk blouse she was wearing with her conservative linen suit was slightly, just slightly, low cut. She hadn't noticed it before, it was only when she leaned forward. But at that moment she felt the presence of her own body in a new way, and now in this Italian restaurant, she had actually just shivered, of all things, she really had, when he leaned across the table and touched her wrist. She'd been pouring the wine and she'd spilled a couple of drops of red wine onto the red and white tablecloth and he'd seen and come to her aid and had leaned forward and held her wrist to steady it, that was all, no, not all, he stared into her eyes as he touched her wrist. She'd never been brought up to want beautiful men. She'd been brought up to want a dentist or a doctor or a lawyer, someone not beautiful, someone hard-working and ordinary. For some reason, she'd always figured it would be the dentist and sometimes she would vividly imagine him, he would have a pleasant sense of humor and play squash, but he was definitely not the kind of man that women became obsessed with, followed around, called at all hours of the night, or died for. . . . He was a trim, nice, happy, safe dentist. And what could Michael teach her about love that the dentist couldn't? Everything, she knew. If she could only give in, she might finally learn what she'd always wanted to learn. Or would this irrational fear of dying stop her from going home with him tonight and tomorrow, and next week, and next month, no matter how well they got to know each other, no matter how many Italian dinners they shared, but it wasn't an irrational fear, it was a perfectly rational fear. After all, she hadn't invented the disease. She was innocent. But it was so strange to have to think of death and sex together all the time. Sex leads to death. *Could lead to death*, she reminded herself. Doesn't necessarily. And it wasn't as though she was at high risk. She was at much higher risk of getting breast cancer because her mother and her mother's sister had had mastectomies, although both were doing terrifically now, thank goodness. But she couldn't do much about preventing that, could she? Watch her diet, get frequent check-ups, but sex was a different story. You could be careful. You could abstain. You could put potential lovers through a lie detector test. Because sex could lead to death. *Could.* With the wrong person. Doesn't necessarily, but one night, just one night with the wrong person. . . . She looked at Michael. *What a beauty*, it was impossible to associate him with the Grim Reaper, but maybe his beauty meant he was the Angel of Death. But he was a singer, which meant he had music inside of him, not death. Besides, wouldn't she be willing to expire in his arms in exchange for the greatest passion of her life? Yes. Maybe. If she could be guaranteed that he would love her deeply and that a night with him would be so beautiful and romantic and special that nothing else would seem worth living for afterwards, if like Juliet she could inspire generations of lovers to come. But Juliet had not lain for months in a hospital bed, feeble and emaciated and delirious. Yet, why was Michael any less worth dying for than Romeo? Was he really any less safe?

Marissa looked nothing like the women Michael was usually attracted to, who were dark and vampy looking, actually, in some cases, more like vampires than vamps, always dressed in black with cruel red mouths and long black hair with thick bangs that covered their foreheads and made their mascaraed eyes look like mean little slits. These women came on to him at clubs, because they liked the way he moved on stage in the tight leather pants he wore as part of the act, but which he never wore offstage. Yet from the first moment in the real estate office, he'd been drawn to perky blonde Marissa in her proper suit and silk blouse, the way she smelled of some violet perfume, she looked so sweet and well groomed, the kind of girl his mother would approve of, very pretty, she could be on TV advertising dishwashing lotion. In the past, Marissa would not have interested him at all, he knew, but he'd changed this past year, since he'd lost his friend Haruki. It hadn't been a deliberate or manipulative change, it was just that losing Haruki that way, so suddenly, so tragically, had made him stop short and rethink everything about himself. And that included his desire for the vampire women. And when he saw Marissa this morning he'd seen in her something so sweet, so yearning, so untouched. She was beautiful, and it was her very sweetness that was like a light beckoning him. The appeal of the women before had been that they knew all about sex and lust and passion, that they craved it and coveted it, that they weren't the type to marry and settle down, something he certainly hadn't dreamed of doing until later, maybe when he was thirty-five or so. But now people were dying. People he knew. And he was at high risk, maybe. Maybe not. But he'd been with the vampire women, lots of them, and he'd been with two men, also, years ago. When he'd first graduated from college and moved to the city and started singing at clubs.

Before anyone knew about the disease, before anyone had gotten sick and died, before sex and death became linked. No big deal in either case, he'd thought at the time. He traveled in daring circles, wild circles, circles that didn't care about conventionality, about sexual stereotypes. Paul, who worked with him at the deli and who went to clubs at night and who reminded him of the perennial muscular All-American football hero, had flirted with him for awhile, and then had come to hear him play one night at a club and after the show Paul invited him back to his place in Park Slope for a drink and it was early dawn when they got there, and Michael thought, why not, so many men, and women, too, had homoerotic experiences. You did it a few times in your youth, like a kind of ritual among those who were sensual and open-minded, among those not totally hung up in stifling sexual stereotyping. And it hadn't been amazing, it hadn't been awful, it had been that balance that sex often turned out to be, in reality, even with the vampire women, some of whom removed their black dresses and red lipstick and then wanted to get married after all. With Marv it had been different. He'd felt affection for Marv, he'd cared for him, and it wasn't a whim, it had been building for a while. Marv was an editor at a magazine that looked at hot trends around downtown and he hung out at clubs to get story ideas, and they'd been meeting on and off, and then one day they went home together and then for a week they got together every single night and then Marv said he was falling in love with Michael and Michael knew that he was in dangerous territory, too dangerous for him, the kind of danger where someone kind would get very hurt if he didn't act forthrightly and decisively and he did, he was honest and said that he didn't feel that way and they should just stop it, and although Marv took it well, and said he understood and appreciated Michael's honesty, they didn't stay friends. Marv stopped coming to the clubs, and Michael had to tell himself that nevertheless what he had done was a good thing. Because he couldn't love Marv, probably could never love a man, although he hated to make categorical statements like that, but well, it was the kind of thing you knew about yourself, it wasn't a matter of politics. And now he wondered about them both. A lot. About Paul and Marv, especially Marv. Were they safe? Were they alive and infected, or alive and healthy? Alive and healthy and scared to death and watching their loved ones die around them? Paul, he knew, had moved away about a year before, had gone back to the Midwest somewhere, Michael couldn't remember exactly which state, Iowa, Nebraska, maybe, to take over his father's business and to help take care of his father who was dying of an old man's disease. Marv was still listed in the phone book, Michael had looked him up, and he knew that he could call Marv at any time just to say, "I loved you as a friend, now I worry about you, I think about you." But he didn't, he didn't want to upset Marv and he didn't want to know him in any way but the way he'd known him, alive, handsome, vibrant. But now he was living in fear himself simply because he had wanted to know something different and unique in his lifetime, something that hadn't seemed ugly to him, still didn't seem ugly to him, the way it had to the guys at college, but then so many of those guys had called not only homosexuals by the most vile names, but women and blacks, too, anyone not exactly like them, and he'd never been like those guys, he'd never wanted to be like them. His sin was that he had an imagination, not a lack of one. His sin was that he'd valued sensuality, that he'd loved the vampire women, and two good men. And a test wouldn't tell him much, would just upset him. If it were negative, he'd think it was wrong, a mistake, and he'd probably spend every few months coming back, getting retested, becoming obsessed, and if it was positive, all it would mean, really, was that he had been exposed to the disease at some point, and being exposed didn't mean that you would ever get the disease, but it did mean you could give someone else the disease, but no matter what, whether you tested positive, negative, or off the map, if you were a caring, decent person, you would try to be safe from here on in, anyway, so why take the test? You might test positive and live to the ripe old age of ninety, or you might test negative and be hit by a car on your way home from the test, or you might test negative this week and positive in ten weeks. On the other hand, maybe taking the test was necessary, another ritual. He didn't know, but in any case, he'd been feeling half-dead already, not sexual, not curious, not even when he was on stage in leather and singing, he was just going through all the motions, ever since Haruki had died. Haruki had come to the states with his family when he was in his teens, they were wealthy, his father owned a Japanese restaurant on the Upper East Side known for its sushi bar, for its oyster sushi and caviar sushi, and Michael had met Haruki through one of the members of his band who ate sushi at the restaurant. Haruki lived near the deli and they grew close. Haruki had become his best friend, if you allowed yourself to think like that, in terms of best friends and second best friends, all that teenage stuff. But Haruki was his best friend, really, they'd gotten that close. Haruki was a social worker at a hospital and all day long he worked with men who were dying, he tried to get them social services, tried to make them more comfortable, tried to comfort their families, and although he worked with some women he said it was, naturally, mostly men, and he talked about the pain and frustration of trying to make the last days of dying young men better, and he said there were the middle-class men who wanted to talk to him about their fears and needs and loves, and then there were the poor men, usually black and Hispanic, who didn't want to talk at all, but then sometimes after acting tough and mean for weeks or months they would ask Haruki to please just sit quietly at their bedside for an hour, to please read to them from a newspaper. . . . And then Haruki, who'd lived with one man, Jaime, a psychotherapist, for five years, had come down with the disease himself and died. After Haruki's death Michael couldn't imagine love without imagining death, but now around Marissa he felt alive again, aroused, desirous. She was pouring the sweet red wine, he saw her hand tremble, saw her spill a little and he leaned forward to steady her wrist, and the way her skin felt, and the way she looked at him, as though she were awakening from a deep sleep, like Sleeping Beauty, which made him Prince Charming, which was corny, nothing like what went on between him and the vampire women who scorned fairy tales except maybe ones about bloodsucking vampires, and he felt excited and happy and unnerved and tense all at the same time and he needed to release the tension. With Marissa. In her arms. Tonight. He had to look down and stop meeting her gaze. How could he be with her? He wasn't sure he was safe, and undoubtedly, she so sweet, so innocent, she had to be safe, but why? Being blonde and perky was no guarantee. This disease wasn't moral or judgmental. It was a virus, a random, hideous, ugly virus, and he refused to think that ill people were bad people, sordid people. He'd wanted Marissa so much, though, all day, since the morning visit to the real estate office, he'd been thinking about her, he'd felt happier than he had in ages. It had been such a long time since he wanted someone so much. He felt filled with longing, and he loved the feeling. Her spirit intrigued him, captivated him, he sensed that she'd been holding back a passion within herself, a wildness, a ferocity, an ability to love deeply and daringly, and that she too needed a release, and he wanted to be that release for her.

Marissa thought: I want to know obsessive love just once. I want to feel wild and driven, jealous and possessive and anxious and exhilarated and inventive and crazed with love. I want to dream of him at night, to know that he is dreaming of me, mad, uncontrollable dreams, and I want to know that he desires me all the time, I want to live in a long delirious sensual fog, just once. Once. Before settling down with the safe dentist. Or maybe, she lifted her eyes to look at Michael, instead of settling down with the dentist. Maybe she and Michael would kill off the dentist together tonight. Maybe it was the dentist who wasn't safe tonight.

Michael thought: we'll do it safely, we can make love safely, perfectly, love can be safe. He knew the rules and
regulations. He'd read so many articles and he and Haruki
had spoken at length about dos and don'ts. Yet Haruki had
died, despite knowing all the rules and regulations. But love
could still be safe. The world hadn't stopped making love
because of the disease, although, in a way, it was true, the
world *had* stopped making love, whole worlds of people,
whole solar systems and galaxies had stopped making love
to each other. And some of the articles said that there was
no safe lovemaking at all. The President had gone on record saying that only abstinence was safe, but screw the
President, that was crazy. He wasn't going to his grave
never knowing love again. What was so very precious
about his life that he needed to hold onto it at all costs,
even at the cost of hardly living at all? And then he couldn't
resist. He leaned over and touched her wrist again. This time
she wasn't pouring the wine. He just held her wrist, her skin
was so fresh, she seemed to inhale, to flush, and it made him
want her so much. He had a friend, Bob, in his late thirties,
who had gone through the sixties, he'd been a hippie with
hair to his ass and had worn those shirts with American
flags sewn into them. He'd taken lots of LSD, had "balled
lots of chicks," as he put it, but nowadays he was married
and had a computer business and short hair, and he was
always saying he was so glad that he was ten years older
than Michael and that he'd been young during the sixties
and had balled around before the disease. There had been
crabs and the clap back then, sure, he told Michael, but they
were nothing, inconveniences, easily dealt with, just a quick
trip to the free clinic, and the clinic was a cool place to go
to, guys didn't mind going there, since that was where the
chicks went to get their birth control pills. Bob would say
that in those days if you had clap or crabs it meant you
were liberated, it was a kind of medal or badge, condoms
were passé then, a part of a creepy repressed American past
featuring clumsy, terrified kids in the back seats of cars. The
hippie days had changed that, teenagers made love boldly,

in front of each other, they explored their sensuality, Bob
said. Michael had always thought the hippie experience was
naive and silly, but these days he wasn't so sure. "I made it
with chicks whenever I wanted to," Bob said, "and it wasn't
sordid or silly, that's today's media trying to tell you it was
like that, but we really are the love generation and we were
beautiful, and it's you I feel sorry for, for your generation,"
and then he would pause, look around at his big house, his
elaborate computers, his pretty wife, and say, "I had it all
back then, and I have it all now, because I'm safe."

For years Marissa had been watching sexy women in films
and on TV, and while they were motivated by wild passion,
she felt none, in her world of high school cheerleaders and
college sorority sisters, love was always discussed in terms
of security and material goods, never passion and lust. She
suspected that other women had secrets, that they were
more womanly than she was, she felt like white bread
in a world of exotic loaves. At her health club, where
she took aerobics classes four mornings a week before
work, she watched the women in the locker room as
they got dressed, and she wondered which ones knew
about passion, and sometimes she even wondered which
ones were into the kinky stuff she'd read about, slaves and
masters and leather, but mostly she just wondered which
ones knew pure passion. She would stare suspiciously at
the ones stepping into sexy black lace panties, rolling black
fishnet pantyhose up their legs, and she would imagine that
they were the biggest phonies of all, desperately trying to
buy sexuality by copying lingerie ads, she imagined that
they, like her, sat behind desks at offices wishing they could
come alive. But there was one woman Marissa saw often, a
swimmer, and she wore men's cotton briefs and undershirts
beneath her jeans and sweaters and she laughed a lot and
sometimes she put on pale lipstick, but that was it, no
rouge or perfume, and then she would dash off, barely
remembering to brush her hair, always in a great hurry,
and Marissa would study her, certain that she genuinely

knew passion in men's arms, that she was rushing off to
fling herself into a lover's arms, that she easily allowed
herself to be transformed by desire, by love. Sometimes
Marissa would turn away from the woman, embarrassed
by such thoughts, and then other times she wanted to tap
her on the shoulder as she was zipping up her jeans and ask,
"Why you? Why not me?" and then other times she wanted
to say, "Teach me to be that way, to abandon myself, to feel
loved and loving." But now she was released from that envy,
in a way, wasn't she? Because she was safe, and that woman
might not be. She was sure she was safe. No need to take
a test. Short of having lived in a nunnery or having been
sealed in a bubble, it would be almost impossible to be safer
than she was. Unless you were already dead.

Michael thought about Haruki's death, about how Haruki
had always spoken so freely about loving men, even when it
had caused his traditional family great pain, but he refused
to hide it, and they loved him, he was still Haruki, their son,
their brother, and they came around. At the end, in his
hospital bed, during his third and final stay in the hospital,
Haruki, who had cared for the dying, was wizened and aged
and needed taking care of himself. On Haruki's best days
Michael thought he looked like an old Oriental sage, but that
was just a dream-image, in fact, Haruki looked terrible, he
could hardly breathe or keep food down, he was emaciated,
bald, only sometimes lucid. At the end, fewer and fewer
people came to the hospital to visit him. Haruki's lover,
Jaime, never stopped coming, and his father and mother and younger sister never stopped. And Michael never
stopped. But even his brother came less and less, and there
was one woman from the social work unit at the hospital
who came, but most of his co-workers had stopped fairly
early. And even so Haruki had more visitors than so many
of the men. "I've made my peace with dying," Haruki said to
Michael the week before he died, "I feel no guilt, no regrets.
Hardly any fear." But Haruki's sister had turned to Michael
in the hospital cafeteria one evening as they stood together

on line, each buying a cup of chicken soup to eat at Haruki's bedside, and she'd said to him fiercely, "How will I ever lie in anyone's arms and feel free and safe and loving again? Haruki has destroyed me." Michael had been speechless, he knew he needed to say something, to defend Haruki and to reassure his sister, and yet he understood her pain and her rage so deeply, knew that she wouldn't be easily reassured, and he felt inadequate. "No, you're okay," he finally shrugged, feeling barely verbal, like an inarticulate character in a bad gangster film. He and Haruki's sister had ridden up the hospital elevator silently together, not looking at each other, and they sat side by side at Haruki's bedside sipping their bland chicken soup from paper cups, watching Haruki sleep a troubled sleep, and Michael's entire sexual life passed before his eyes, he remembered details and nuances he'd completely forgotten about, as though it were he and not Haruki who was dying. Or else he and Haruki dying together. "I wanted," he whispered after a while, after they'd both finished their soup, "to know love of many sorts." "Yes, I know," Haruki's sister whispered back somberly, nodding at her brother, "so did he, and look at him now." "But he loved well," Michael whispered, thinking of Jaime's devotion. "Did he?" she asked. And then the co-worker from the social work unit at the hospital came, and he and Haruki's sister never had a chance to speak again. A week later Haruki was dead. At the funeral, Michael hugged her, but he sensed how separate and alone the grief of a sister made her, and when she looked at him Michael thought, she doesn't have any idea who I am.

Marissa thought: does he want me as much as I want him? Does he find me as beautiful as I find him? He couldn't possibly. I'm much more ordinary than he is. Does he anticipate my kisses, the taste of my lips and my flesh? Somehow she knew that he did. She thought of a film she'd seen recently, in which the heroine, a bold, sexy, fleshy woman, stands naked above the hero, who's lying in bed. In awe, he looks up at her, this goddess. And then she seems to recognize her own power, to marvel at his lust and awe. And Marissa had held her breath during the entire scene. And that was how it would be with Michael. She would do what the woman in the film did, she would stand above Michael naked and proud, liberated and reckless. Except, how could she? How could she risk dying just to mimic some actress in a film? After all, she didn't know whether Michael was safe.

Michael leaned forward in the seat and his knee brushed against Marissa's, and he saw her expression change, come alive, and he thought, there is no way, no way on this earth, that Marissa and I will not go home together tonight. This is extraordinary. I cannot let her go. We'll make love, we'll do it safely, we'll follow guidelines. And then he thought, no, we won't follow all the guidelines, if we follow them all, we won't be making love, we'll be doing exercises, going through mere motions. Love must be transforming, I must know her intimately. But if we don't follow guidelines, will she be safe? Will I? He reached over and took her hand in his, took her fingers in his hand and held them lightly. This time his touch was deliberate and unambiguous, he was definitely holding her hand in order to touch her, not merely helping her pour the wine.

Oh, she thought, this is lovely, perfect, like my dreams, his touch is so different than Buddy's, than Harry's, than those men I dated, with their mundane touches, their leaden fingers. Michael's fingers were small flames, and she imagined those fiery fingers touching her belly and then touching between her thighs and she couldn't breathe. "Love me," she thought, "love me." sometimes those words went through her mind at night before she fell asleep, but they just floated out into the air because there was nobody in the room with her, but now for the first time they were directed at someone, at this man across the table, Michael. She tossed her hair back, even though she wore it in a short layered bob and it was hardly tossable.

The waiter came and placed the check in front of Michael. Michael could tell that Marissa intended to split it with him. Well, after all, it hadn't really been a date. But he wanted to pay for her dinner, to pay for her everywhere, forever, even though he worked in a deli and hardly made any money singing with the band at the clubs, and she worked in real estate and made lots more money than he did, he didn't care, he wanted to pay for her everywhere, forever, but he didn't know how to say so, without feeling foolish, a parody of a protective father figure, and he didn't want to establish that role with her, so he didn't say anything and they each paid half of the bill. But over time, he thought, he would take care of her and he would respect her, treasure her, continue to desire her, and teach her about love.

They stood in the street outside the restaurant. He wanted to say, let's share a taxi together back to my place, please come home with me because if we make love tonight I promise you that it will be more beautiful than all the love you've read about in books or seen in movies, and it will last a lifetime or longer and it will change us both, I promise you, and we may never feel like this again, so please come home with me tonight, let's give the taxi driver just one address.

She wanted to say, I need to find the courage to go home with you, because you are the lover I've yearned for my whole life, I need to be strong tonight and not worry about the dentist and the house in the suburbs, because the dentist will never look at me in awe, and you will, I need to say to you, let's take a taxi together and then let's go to bed together, I need so much to sit beside you in the taxi and to feel your knee brush against mine, to feel your arm around my shoulder, to know that we are going home to one destination. . . .

"I'll just hail a taxi here," she said, outside the restaurant, "and I'll call you when apartments come up that seem right for you." Her voice was too polite. "A taxi?" he asked, thinking, her voice is so cool, so distant, how can that be, why is she choosing to leave me tonight, to go home alone? "Yes," she said, thinking, I've made my choice and I may live to regret it, but you are too beautiful, too open, too vulnerable, I love all that about you, but I want the dentist and the security too much, and I hope that you will forgive me. She said, "I live on a very good block and my building has a doorman, so if I hail a taxi and take it right to my door, I'll be perfectly safe. I always am."

JUST ONE LOOK

You look at other women. It's difficult enough to be faithful with your body, let alone with your mind, and so you look. You feel okay about it, it's not as if you find yourself in bed with everyone you see: you just look, you can't help but notice the woman in the very short blue-jean cut-offs. It's normal, relax, you assure yourself each time you start to feel a smidgen of guilt.

You woke up this morning, dreaming of someone other than the person with whom you share breakfast, dinner, the shower, the rent. It's no big deal, you tell yourself, it's natural, it's life. Maybe you miss a little of the excitement of being single, you think, but only a little. Other times you think it's a shame that you met her when you were still so young, before you had your chance to experiment, to sow oats, to taste life.

Now as you stroll down the street, you find yourself watching a pigeon flying overhead, and that old song goes through your mind—what are the words again?—something about wishing you could be as free as the bird up high. . . . But you think you're just being nostalgic, or corny.

Then you see a couple walking down the street. You note the man noting another woman. Suddenly, your heart opens up and you experience something new. Empathy? You're not sure, but you start to wonder what his woman thinks about when she sees him staring lasciviously at another woman. You try to become his woman in order to understand, and you wonder, should you be jealous, sad, angry, betrayed, understanding, disinterested? Should you plot revenge, or should you try to discuss it rationally during dinner? Should you excuse it? After all, it's the first time. . . . Or should you excuse it because he does it all the time, he can't help himself, it doesn't mean anything?

Then you wonder, well, how did the other woman feel, the one who was ogled, knowing that the man who ogled her was with another woman. You try to become the other woman then, for the moment. Are you terribly flattered, flattered even more than when a man alone makes you aware of his interest? Should you be pleased that you wooed him away from his true love, that you were attractive enough to do that without even trying? Does it bode well for your future? Or should you be mad as can be, finding it disgusting that they can't even control their piggish ways when they're with their wives.

Then you try to become the man, himself. You wonder if you're even aware of what you just did, of how you allowed your eyes to turn completely away from your woman, allowing them to turn toward the breasts of this tan, blonde girl in her sheer tube top. Are you aware that you followed her with your eyes for quite some time? A full minute, perhaps, the kind of minute that small children elongate by counting One Mississippi, Two Mississippi. . . . Are you aware that you broke off what you were saying mid-sentence? Do you even remember what you'd been saying? Are you aware that your woman watched you as you watched her, watched as your eyes veered downward to better glimpse her rear, as she turned the corner? Did you see your woman's lips turn grim just briefly? Did you do the whole damned thing on purpose, anyway?

Then you realize that there is a ravaged bag lady on the corner who witnessed the whole event. This thing your heart is insisting upon doing makes you become her, too. An old lady with fading dreams and varicose veins . . . sitting on a curb, surrounded by ripped shopping bags. Once you had been a debutante. Do you remember your youth, the delicate white gown, the lavender corsage, the carefully tweezed eyebrows, the dates with Bif and Bo and Bic? Do you feel enraged, do you despise this vulgar, crass world? Are you glad that you decided to step aside, that you're not part of the mainstream any longer? Do you remember—against your will—the time you saw Bif ogle your little sister in the parlor? Or do you think incoherently, in mystical witch-like mumbo jumbo, about eyes, hell, damnation, cursed flesh and ruination?

Without even a pause, then, you find yourself becoming the policeman sitting in the car stopped for a red light. Face it, everyone on that corner was watching and felt something! That man who noted the other woman simply could not have been more obvious! And now that you're receptive, you have no choice but to become them all. You force yourself to think calmly for a minute . . . you're not an ordinary cop, although you did attend Police Academy, even went to John Jay College for a year or two. You fit inside your uniform well, you have a loving wife, three children, a good religious upbringing. But deep in your heart, you wish you were a woman. Plain and simple. So what do you think, finally, as you watch the man watch the woman? That everyone's a goddamned hypocrite, and then you feel sick because you, yourself, are the worst of the lot! You slam your foot down on the accelerator when the light turns green, and you worry that your partner might be starting to grow suspicious of your chronic moodiness.

Anyway, by now you're feeling terribly obsessive. Not to mention paranoid. First you were watching someone else, but by now you feel that everyone is watching you while you watch them watch him, and her, and each other, and you.

You're confused, so you remind yourself that sure, occasionally, you have taken a peek or two, and yes, you've also had a few vivid and detailed dreams. But does that merit this guilt, this fear? you ask. Well, a voice deep inside you responds, where does harmless looking end and genuine need begin? Doesn't the drug addict rationalize in the same way?

Addicted for sure, you realize, because the very next second you're in the mind of the professor of psychology watching through the grocery store window. Jumbled thoughts of Freud, toilet training, mothers and wombs. You find yourself wishing that you'd had a better glimpse of the woman who'd been watched . . . it would help you to have keener insight into the moment. Suddenly you remember your older sister's thighs . . . which brings you up short.

Whoa, you say, where does this all lead? Worry lines engrave themselves in your brow. You remember the analogy of the drug addict. Nothing optimistic to think about there.

You'll just quit, you decide, really quit. Just like that. Cold turkey! No more looking. That simple. Not even once more, not a peek, not a glimpse. No. You'll wear imaginary blinders. You'll inform your friends that they must never, never try to tempt you. You'll tell them that you've had an experience of sorts. . . . They won't question you much, they'll be too frightened. After all, they've experienced it too.

But dreams! The dreams . . . now you grow truly afraid. How can you stop the dreams? Well, you can't and that's that. You just can't. Remember the addict! Remember! Each morning now when you wake up from a dream which you hadn't intended to have, which you therefore had against your will because you are weak and mortal and flesh and blood and flawed . . . you will feel so damned guilty, so lousy, so rotten. . . . You'll experience pure terror and self-loathing. You'll constantly rue the day that you looked at the man who reminded you of yourself as he looked at the woman. And every day like that will find you receptive to others out there, all those others always watching, watching. And you know already, don't you, that there's simply no turning back. Your eyes will see, you will lust, and your heart will break.

VANNA

As usual, my wife Val and I met after work at the fountain in the center of the Nelson A. Rockefeller Empire State
Plaza in downtown Albany, where the State office buildings are
located. She smiled at me, and I smiled back, but we didn't kiss
hello. I made it a point never to kiss her in public. After all, we
weren't a couple of wacko teenagers obsessed with touching
each other's bodies.

Val and I strolled on over to Lark Street, where there
was a strip of restaurants. Most of them were overpriced,
with shiny plastic plants in all the windows and waiters with
phony accents. We didn't eat out much, but once in a while,
for a treat, we went to a small place called the Waffle Shop
which wasn't overpriced like the fancy places. Lots of State
workers went there.

We had to wait a few minutes for a table. Val was pretty quiet while we waited on line, but that was typical. She wasn't much of a talker. I liked that about her.

Finally, the waitress, one of those wacko types with two earrings in one ear and no earrings in the other, seated us at a table way in the back.

I settled in and looked at the menu. I decided to order number twenty-six, the Mexican waffle with avocado, sour cream, melted cheese, and salsa. Sometimes Mexican food didn't agree with me, but I felt like taking a chance.

Val seemed distracted, and I guessed that she was probably having some trouble with her boss. Sometimes when he complained that she wasn't fast or accurate enough on the word processor, she would come home slightly distracted for a day or two. But she always snapped out of it pretty quickly.

The wacko waitress came over to take our order. She wasn't wearing a bra, and she was wearing a sleeveless pink shirt you could see right through. My eyeglasses, which were loose, started to slide down my nose. I'd been meaning to get them tightened. I pushed them up. The waitress's breasts were rounder than Val's, I noticed. Although I couldn't be absolutely sure. When Val and I made love, we did some kissing and hugging, and then I got on top, and we kept the lights off, so I never got to see too much of her breasts. I looked at the waitress again. She was probably the type who liked porno magazines and electrical devices and did it standing on her head.

"Val?" I asked, trying to ignore both the waitress's breasts and the fact that my eyeglasses were sliding down my nose again, "ready to order?"

The waitress just stood there and played with her hair, which was standing up in little spikes all around her head. She looked as though she'd just stuck her finger into an electrical outlet.

"Oh, I'll have number one," Val said, sounding even more distracted. Number one was just the plain waffle. Nothing on it. Usually she ordered number eight, the waffle with peanut butter and sliced bananas, or number three, the pizza waffle.

"Feeling okay?" I asked. I was relieved that the waitress had gone.

Val leaned forward. She was wearing one of my favorite dresses of hers. She'd sewed it herself. It was a shiny rayon with small yellow flowers on it, and she'd tied a matching shiny yellow ribbon through her shoulder-length brown hair. "Peter," she said, "I had this . . . flash . . . today about what's wrong with my life."

Flash? It wasn't like Val to use a word like that. It was a word a wacko would use. The waitress probably used it when she was in bed with one of her wacko lovers. "I'm flashing," she would say. And then she would groan. Val and I hardly ever groaned. Just then, the waitress brought over our waffles. I refused to look at her breasts this time because I didn't want to give her the satisfaction. The only reason she was wearing a blouse like that in the first place was just so that people would look. Instead, I looked down at my number twenty-six waffle. The avocado slices looked awfully green and oily.

"I had a flash, yes," Val said, staring at her plain waffle. "I'm in the wrong job."

I calmed down. I took a bite of the avocado. A little too spicy, maybe, for my taste, but not really oily. Pretty good, in fact. I took another bite. Val and I had been married almost two years, and even in the most ordinary lives, I told myself, there were bound to be minor crises. It was only natural that one of us would eventually want a new job. Personally, I liked being a computer programmer for the state. "Maybe you could transfer to another office," I said.

"Peter, you're not getting it. It's not a question of switching offices," Val said. "It's bigger than that. It's the whole thing. Petty bureaucrats. Civil servants. Peter, listen to me," she began cutting her waffle into tiny pieces, "I'm meant for something bigger!"

I looked over at the next table. A bald fellow I saw a lot in the elevator of Building One was eating a waffle with a slice of chicken breast on it. I peeked at the menu. It was number twenty-seven. I wished I'd ordered it. I was suddenly starting to feel pretty queasy.

"I wasn't meant to be a word processor," Val said. She had a piece of waffle on her fork and was waving it around. "I was meant to be a performance artist."

So that was it. Back in college for about a week she'd had this same wacko idea that she was going to be an actress. I'd forgotten all about it because it had seemed so unlike her. But now it came back to me, "Val, wait a second," I said, "remember that time when you tried out for the role of Laura in *The Glass Menagerie* and the drama teacher said that your performance was enough to make the audience as emotionally crippled as Laura was? Remember?" I wished I'd brought some antacid tablets with me. My stomach was making noises.

"I don't mean an *actress*, Peter. I don't want to recite lines written by someone else. I said I wanted to be a performance artist!"

So maybe the emphasis was on the artist part, not the performance part, I thought. "But Val," I said, trying to stifle a belch, "you can't draw a straight line."

"Peter, really, not a visual artist," she sighed. "I'm telling you that I've known since we were first married that I was meant for great things. I'm meant to be a performance artist." She pressed her lips together. "Like Laurie Anderson. You know."

"Laurie Anderson?" I thought for a moment. "She's a unit director over at the Office of Mental Health, right?"

"Peter," she said, "really." And she began singing some strange song about Superman and a judge in a really tiny voice, and she sounded like one of the Munchkins from *The Wizard of Oz.*

But I couldn't, for the life of me, imagine Laurie Anderson from Mental Health singing like a Munchkin.

"Or like Eric Bogosian, you know."

I tried to place him. Bogosian. Bogosian. One of the salesmen at the shoestore at the mall was named Eric, but I didn't remember him having such an ethnic last name.

Val began shouting out the name Sid at the top of her lungs over and over again. She seemed to be imitating someone. Maybe she was imitating Muriel Rosenbloom, the mother of her college roommate, Nancy Rosenbloom. Nancy's father was named Sid. I'd met Muriel and Sid once, at Nancy's wedding in Long Island. But why in the world was Val doing an imitation of Muriel Rosenbloom?

The bald fellow with the number twenty-seven chicken-breast waffle was staring at us. In fact, lots of familiar faces from the State Plaza were staring at us. I stifled a belch.

The waitress came over to clear our table. She was smiling at Val. "Great," she said, "those were great Anderson and Bogosian imitations. Are you a performance artist?"

Val gave me an I-Told-You-So look. She said, "Sort of," to the waitress. I asked for the check. People were still looking at us. I wanted out of there quick.

Val didn't say anything else. We left the Waffle Shop and walked the few blocks back to the parking lot at the Plaza. During the ride home, Val just kept looking out the car window, and my stomach kept making noises and I kept stifling belches, which were getting louder and louder all the time.

The minute we got upstairs I rushed to the bathroom and took six antacid tablets. I chewed them down, not even minding the chalk taste. Then I got undressed and put on my brown and white checkered pajamas, which Val had given me for our first anniversary. When I walked into the bedroom, Val was sitting very calmly on the bed, her head against the pillows, already in her pink seersucker pajamas, my anniversary gift to her. "Want to watch TV?" I asked. TV would calm her down, I was sure, and this whole flash thing would pass. I sat down on the edge of the bed.

"No," she said, looking at me. "I don't want to watch TV. I've got a videotape I want to play for you." She got out of bed and went across the room to her bureau and pulled out a tape from her top drawer.

"What is it?" I tried to act as though it were the most natural thing in the world for her to have rented a movie for the VCR on her own.

Val popped the tape into the VCR, and while it was winding, she said, "This is a tape of a performance-art festival that was held a couple of months ago at an East Village club."

"An East Village club?" I asked. How did she know anything about clubs in the East Village? We never even visited
New York. "Albany is a big enough city for me, thank you,"
she'd said last year to Babs, one of the other word proces-
sors in her office, when Babs had invited her to drive into
Manhattan to take in a Broadway play. But I'd heard plenty
about the East Village. It was filled with wackos of every size,
color, and sex.

"The first artist you'll see is B. Morrison creating a character called Banana Medley," Val said.

Val got back into bed. We sat side by side, our heads
against the pillows. It felt so comfortable and familiar that I
almost expected to see Johnny Carson and Ed McMahon up
there on the screen. But just then the picture came on and
some sort of short-haired creature was standing on an empty
stage. The quality of the picture was lousy, and I couldn't tell
whether the creature was male or female, fifteen years old or
a hundred. All I could tell was that it was dressed in some sort
of slinky yellow jumpsuit.

"Now just watch," Val said, not taking her eyes off the
screen.

The creature began to sing, "I'm Chiquita Banana and I'm
here to say . . ." I still couldn't tell, not even from its voice,
what sex this B. Morrison who was "creating the character"
of Banana Medley was. "Now I will do my banana dance for
you," it said. It began to jump and hop around the stage. Then
someone backstage threw it a real banana. It caught the banana and began to wave it around making obscene gestures with
it, putting it near its groin and grunting. Then it dropped the
banana on the stage and walked off, holding its nose.

"Val," I said, "I don't get it."

"Peter, really," she sighed. "That was about how most
people are uptight and scared, and how they need to loosen
up a little."

"What a wacko idea," I said.

She shook her head impatiently. "Just watch. The next
artist is Mike Good. He's creating his greatest character, Mikey
Marine. This piece is about the horrors of war."

I decided to keep my mouth shut this time.

So this guy came out on stage. I could tell this one was definitely a male. He was dressed in a Marine outfit and he had a gun at his side. He started doing a tap dance. He began speaking in a low voice. "I'm Mikey Marine," he said. "I'm a fighting machine, yesirree." He was really light on his feet. Then he started running around in circles yelling, "Kill the Gooks," and cocking his gun. Then he fell to the floor and began writhing around, yelling, "My arm, ouch, there goes my arm, ouch, there goes my other arm, ouch, there goes my leg, ouch, there goes my other leg," and then he screamed at the top of his lungs, "ouch, goddamnit, there go my balls!"

I had had it. I grabbed the remote control switch and shut the VCR off. The screen went blank. "Val, what the heck was that wacko stuff?"

"I told you, Peter. It was performance art." She sighed and began talking to me as though I were a two-year-old. Once in a while Val used to do that. It wasn't one of the things I liked most about her. "In performance art," Val explained, "the artist creates a character and that character *is* the piece. The character is the vehicle through which the performance artist's artistic vision is expressed."

I shook my head. "Listen," I said. "Let's just watch some ordinary TV, okay?" She shrugged, and I turned on an episode of "Miami Vice." It was pretty good, about some Cuban drug dealers. After "Miami Vice," we watched the news and then we watched "The Tonight Show," but Val didn't laugh once, not even when Johnny teased Ed about his weight. After that, I turned out the lights and we went to sleep.

The next week, Val was so distracted, she barely seemed to notice that I was around. She was silent when we drove in to work, silent when we met at the fountain at five o'clock, silent during the drive home, silent during and after dinner. Finally, I said, "Val, honey, please tell me what's wrong."

"Peter," she said matter of factly, "I told you already. I'm going to quit my job and become a performance artist and I've got a lot of thinking to do about creating a character so that I can get my first gig."

Gig? Like *flash*, it wasn't a word Val used. For the rest of
that night, she didn't pay any attention to me at all. Instead,
she just popped that damned tape into the VCR and sat cross-
legged in bed with a spiral notebook open on her lap. She
took notes while she watched, as though she were studying
for a test. I felt like I was being tested, myself, only it wasn't a
clear-cut multiple choice like a civil service exam, and I didn't
like it one bit.

That Friday, Val and I met at the fountain after work,
and she grabbed my arm and spoke fiercely. "Peter," she
said, "I know I'm only beginning and that I can't create a
character as good as Laurie Anderson's androgynous clone
or Eric Bogosian's neurotic Hollywood agent, but I've got to
test my wings. So I've arranged my first gig tomorrow night
at the Waffle Shop."

"The Waffle Shop?" I repeated, sitting down heavily on
the edge of the fountain.

"Yes, the Waffle Shop." She sounded impatient. "Why not?
I've got to start somewhere. They have poetry readings on the
weekends, you know."

No, I didn't know. On weekends, poetry had been about
the last thing on our minds. On Saturday mornings I'd mow
the lawn and Val would buy groceries and cook. Besides, how
many poets lived in Albany, anyway? At most, I figured, three
or four wackos who'd gotten lost on their way to the East
Village. And I was positive that there weren't any performance artists in Albany. I never saw people who looked like
B. Morrison or Mike Good at the State Plaza or the mall.

But I tried to be a good sport and I drove Val to her gig
on Saturday night. She was wearing a pale pink rayon dress
and a matching pink ribbon in her hair and she didn't look
even slightly wacko. While I was looking for a parking space
on Lark Street, it occurred to me that maybe it was a good
thing that she'd arranged this gig, since she was bound to fail.
And then she'd be embarrassed and she'd forget about this performance art nonsense in the same way she'd forgotten about
wanting to be an actress in college. Val was about as much of
a so-called performance artist as I was!

That night there were about two dozen people in the Waffle Shop, which just about filled the place up. I recognized about half of them from the State Plaza and from the mall, including the bald fellow who'd been eating the chicken-breast waffle the night I'd gotten sick from the Mexican waffle. But there also was a handful of people sitting together at a large table in the corner who struck me as wackos. They were probably the crew who attended the poetry readings. They were all skinny, and it didn't matter whether they were male or female, they had that short spiky hair, as though they'd all stuck their fingers into electrical outlets.

Val seemed nervous. She kept running her fingers through her hair. And I felt ridiculous. My glasses kept sliding down my nose and I kept pushing them up. We stood together in the doorway. Neither of us seemed to want to make the first move inside the restaurant. Then that wacko waitress with the two earrings came over and greeted Val with a big hug. She wasn't wearing a bra again and this time her shirt was a pale yellow. Her breasts looked even rounder than the last time. I looked at Val to make sure she was wearing a bra. It was hard to tell, but I was pretty sure she was.

The waitress walked to the front of the restaurant and clapped her hands for silence. Then she said, "Hey, everyone, I know that Albany isn't the East Village, but I also know that there are people here who do keep up with the arts, just as there are people here who don't," and she managed to smile at the wackos and sneer at the State workers at the same time, "and those of you who *do*, have been following the work of such performance artists as Laurie Anderson, Eric Bogosian, B. Morrison and Mike Good. And tonight Albany is honored to have Val, a local girl and performance artist extraordinaire, doing two of her pieces."

The wackos applauded. The State workers kept eating their waffles. I continued to hang back in the doorway, and I told myself that one bad evening in a marriage wasn't the end of the world. One day when Val and I were old and grey we'd tell our grandchildren about this evening and laugh about it together.

Val walked to the front of the restaurant. She cleared her throat. "My first piece is called 'Avocado Rag,'" she said in a tense, high-pitched voice. The waitress handed her a bright green avocado. I hadn't eaten an avocado since I'd gotten sick from the Mexican waffle, and I started feeling queasy again. Val took the avocado and began dancing around with it, doing little bumps and grinds. Even I could tell that this routine was completely borrowed from Banana Medley's "Banana Rag." Every once in a while Val would look down at the avocado as though she couldn't believe that she was really doing this, which was exactly the way I felt. Then she stopped dancing and stood there waiting, but nobody applauded. Most of the State workers were still eating their waffles and not paying any attention, for which I was grateful, and the wacko types were frowning. I figured that they all recognized the take-off on Banana Medley's piece. But Val held her head high and said, "My next piece is called 'War.'" The waitress came over and handed her a broom. Val cocked it like it was a gun and she ran around in circles yelling, "Ouch, I'm dying, ouch, I'm dying." She was really bombing. And even though that was what I'd wanted, I felt sorry for her.

The State workers were ordering coffee and dessert by then, and the wackos all got up and left the restaurant without applauding. After they'd all gone, the waitress went over to Val and said, "Wow, that was interesting," but even I could tell she didn't mean it.

Val came over to me and hung her head. I decided not to rub it in. I just said, trying not to sound too gleeful, "Alrightey, Val, let's head home."

She was completely quiet during the car ride home. All day Sunday she just stayed in bed, and I left her alone, figuring she needed to recuperate. But on Sunday night, while I was getting into bed, she said, "Peter, listen, I can do it, really! I bombed last night because I wasn't ready yet. I hadn't nurtured my own vision long enough. My own character. But I'm getting closer. I feel her inside me." She smiled. "Her name is Vanna."

That week Val didn't go into work at all. She called in sick every day, and every night when I came home from work I'd find her sitting in the living room at the sewing machine. But she never showed me what she was sewing. All I could see was some filmy black fabric. Val never wore black. "I don't want to look like I'm at a funeral," she always said.

On Saturday mornings Val said, "Peter, they're giving me a second chance at the Waffle Shop tonight. And this time I'm ready. Vanna is going to debut tonight." She hesitated. "I think you'll like her."

I must have looked nervous because she said, "Oh, Peter, come on, it's just performance art. It's not real life. She's just a character I'll be using when I perform. I mean, Mike Good has a Ph.D. in history from Harvard. He's not really Mikey Marine. B. Morrison isn't really Banana Medley. She's Barbara Morrison from a family of bankers. And I'm not really Vanna." But a funny expression came over her face, and I wasn't completely reassured.

That night, the same people, were at the Waffle Shop who'd been there the week before. At least it seemed that way to me. The same State workers, including the bald fellow. The wackos all looked like the same ones, too. And naturally the waitress was the same. This time her shirt was a dark blue and I couldn't see into it but I was pretty sure she still wasn't wearing a bra. And she'd stuck a third earring in her ear.

Val was wearing one of her nicest flowered dresses, one she'd worn the year before to her office Christmas party. It was beige with little pink and purple flowers on it. And she was wearing a matching beige ribbon in her hair and matching beige shoes. So she still didn't look like a wacko, which made me feel calmer.

I stood in the doorway again, but almost immediately I began to feel less calm because I could see how confident Val was this time. She didn't even wait to be introduced. She just marched right up to the front of the restaurant and said in a loud, strong voice, "Last week you all saw me attempt to begin my career as a performance artist. Well, I promise you that I've grown since then. I've worked hard, and I've created my own character. Through her, I will express my vision and speak my mind. Her name," she paused dramatically, "is Vanna."

And then she began to undress, moving her body sen-
sually, in a kind of slow-motion striptease. Her eyes traveled
around the room, meeting each of our gazes one by one.
Everyone was watching her, even the State workers, who'd
stopped eating their waffles. I'd never seen Val move like
that. When you kiss, hug, and get on top, you don't usually
include stripteases. I felt as though I were losing my mind.
I imagined myself dragging her out of the restaurant by her
hair. I imagined myself running out the door of the restaurant
and driving away without her. Maybe I'd change my name,
move to a new state, get a new wife. But instead I just stood
silently in the doorway, watching with disbelief as Val went
wacko in public, right in front of me. Everyone else was silent, too, as she stepped out of her dress. Underneath it she
was wearing a short black lacy nightie, and I suddenly knew
what she'd been so busy sewing all those nights. Then she took
off the beige shoes and she threw them, one at a time, into the
audience. A wacko with bright red spiky hair reached out and
caught both of them. He cradled them in his bony arms. Then
the waitress came over and handed Val a pair of lacy black
pantyhose. Val wriggled suggestively into the hose, teasing us
with which parts of her body she allowed us to see and which
parts she kept hidden.

Then the waitress handed Val a pair of pointed black high
heeled shoes. Val stepped into them gracefully, as though she'd
been born to wear such shoes, never even looking down as she
slid her feet inside them. Her feet looked so slender, so sexy.
I'd never seen them look like that. Then she bent over and
picked up her dress from the floor and tossed that into the
audience, too. The bald fellow grabbed for it and pressed it
to his lips. Val stood there proudly in her black costume, her
legs spread wide, hands on her hips. She'd been totally transformed. I had to sit down. Slowly I made my way from the
doorway to the one empty table, which was right next to the
bald fellow's table.

Meanwhile, everyone in the restaurant kept watching
Val, transfixed. The waitress handed her something else. I
strained to see what it was. I hoped that maybe it was an

avocado or a broom, and that she was going to repeat last week's performance and bomb again. But it looked like a whip. Not that I'd ever seen a whip up close. But when Val grabbed it, twirled it for a moment in the air, brought it down and cracked the floor, I knew for sure that it was a whip. I felt chilled.

"Tonight Vanna is a bad girl," Val announced to the audience, and her voice had become transformed also. It wasn't Val's sweet soft voice. It was sultry and harsh at the same time. She cracked the whip on the floor again. I heard a few people gasp. "Tonight Vanna is a bad girl because it feels good to be a bad girl. Because good boys need bad girls." She looked right at me when she said that. "And bad boys need bad girls, too." And then she looked right at the wacko with the red hair who was holding her shoes in his arms. She started cracking the whip again. I leaned over to the next table and grabbed some pieces of chicken breast off the bald fellow's waffle, and I began shoving them into my mouth. I needed the taste of something bland and familiar to calm me down. The bald fellow's eyes were on Vanna, and he didn't even notice.

I chewed the chicken, which, instead of tasting bland and familiar, tasted dry and grainy, and I closed my eyes and stopped watching Vanna. I couldn't take it any more. I heard her crack the whip a few more times and then I heard her sing something about Vanna getting whatever she wants, but my blood was pounding in my ears and I didn't hear any more of her song.

Suddenly the audience began applauding so loudly that I opened my eyes. Val was bowing, and the wackos were all standing and stamping their feet and whistling. The State workers were still sitting. They looked dazed. But when the bald fellow rose and began stamping his feet and whistling and waving Val's beige dress in the air, then all of the State workers stood and began stamping their feet and whistling, too. Everyone in the restaurant was standing and stamping and whistling except me. I just sat watching them in horror and chewing on a piece of dry chicken breast and pushing my glasses up.

Val kept bowing and grinning from ear to ear. I recognized that grin. It was the same grin she'd worn last year when she'd met me at the fountain and announced that she'd gotten a raise.

The waitress walked over to Val and kissed her on the cheek. Val stopping bowing and then she blushed, and I recognized the blush, too. It was the same blush she'd worn the first time I'd held her hand.

Then she gave a little farewell wave to the audience and walked over to my table. I swallowed the last of the chicken breast. She said, "Okay, Peter, let's go. My shoes are killing me." Her voice was Val's, not Vanna's, and I was relieved.

The crowd was still going crazy, but I got up and followed her out the door of the Waffle Shop.

During the ride home, she crossed her legs and I looked at her slender calves in the lacy black pantyhose and for a moment I had the urge to make love to her right there in the car, to pull over and just do it, but I didn't dare. I was relieved when the urge passed, and embarrassed for even having thought such a thing. But Val didn't seem to notice. She just stared out the car window with a little smile on her face.

When we got home, she slipped out of the black nightie and into her pink seersucker pajamas. She fell asleep, still smiling. I lay awake next to her for hours, and I was able to fall asleep only when I reminded myself that a performance artist in Albany couldn't go very far. I mean, it wasn't the East Village. Val would never become famous like Laurie Anderson and Eric Bogosian. At least I could count on that.

She got a second gig the following week at one of the overpriced restaurants on Lark Street. I drove her there. I hid in the restaurant doorway behind a giant plastic plant with waxy green leaves the color of an avocado. Val walked to the front of the restaurant. The audience was made up mostly of State workers again, and they looked like they were in pretty high positions. And when Val began taking off her flowered rayon dress, I steeled myself for Vanna's black nightie and whip routine. But this time Val stripped down to a white ruffled pinafore. And she slipped her feet into little white ankle socks and white patent leather shoes. She began skipping around on stage, speaking in a breathy, childish voice,

"Tonight Vanna is a sweet little innocent. A virginal cherub. Because both bad boys and good boys need good little girls." And she began singing, "On the Good Ship Lollypop."

The audience ate it up. She got another standing ovation. I drove her home and had the same urge to make love to her in the car. Luckily, the urge passed again. As soon as we got home, she changed into her seersucker pajamas, said goodnight in Val's voice, and fell asleep smiling.

At her third gig, at the Lark Street Art Gallery, she did her striptease in front of a painting of a butterfly. She stripped down to a frumpy yellow mu-mu. "Tonight Vanna is a harried housewife," she said in a frazzled voice, "because without her, none of you boys would even be here today, now would you?" The following week, at the annual Lark Street Crafts Fair, Vanna was a glamorously dressed, high-strung television talk show host. The week after that, at the public library, she was a sensitive, introspective poet. But always, when we got home, after the gigs, she spoke to me in Val's voice and slept next to me in Val's pajamas.

When a reporter from the *Knickerbocker News* came to the house and interviewed her, Val explained, "My character, Vanna, can be anyone. Vanna is a chameleon. If I can imagine someone, Vanna can make her real." Then the local TV news did a spot on her, a local filmmaker made a documentary about her, and a local literary magazine printed the text of one of her pieces and called it a masterpiece. And I kept assuring myself that this was still only Albany, and that nobody in the East Village had ever heard of her, and that she was bound to get tired soon of being a big fish in a little sea. And when she realized that she and Vanna had gone as far as they could go, she'd settle down and become a word processor again.

But then one night she got the phone call. I figured it was the manager of another overpriced restaurant on Lark Street calling to book her. But when she hung up, her eyes were glittery. "They want to legitimize performance art," she said to me in a hushed voice. "They're going to bring it to Lincoln Center. Can you imagine? Me and B. Morrison and Mike Good on stage at Lincoln Center?" She sat down on the edge of the sofa. Her expression was soft and dreamy, and it made me nervous.

But I drove her into Manhattan the night of the Performance Arts Festival at Lincoln Center. It was a four-hour ride, and Val didn't say a word the whole time. She just looked out the car window. She was wearing her beige flowered dress and the matching beige hair ribbon and the matching beige shoes. I parked the car, and we walked through the Plaza at Lincoln Center. When we strolled past the fountain, I found myself missing the fountain at the State Plaza. I knew that fountain so well. I felt comfortable with it. Lincoln Center was too big, too fancy, for my taste.

The Avery Fisher Hall auditorium was packed. Nearly every seat in the house was filled. Hundreds of wackos. I tried to spot Laurie Anderson and Eric Bogosian in the crowd, but all the wacko women looked like Laurie Anderson and all the wacko men looked like Eric Bogosian. And, to my surprise, there were just as many silver-haired ladies in elegant mink coats, with silver-haired gentlemen by their sides.

Val went backstage to prepare. She kissed me goodbye. I sat in the front row, where a seat had been reserved for me. My stomach was queasy. The first act was B. Morrison, performing as Banana Medley doing the "Banana Rag." I didn't pay much attention, since I'd seen it so many times on Val's videotape. But the wackos in the audience loved it. They clapped loudly when she finished. The silver-haired ladies and gentlemen, however, sat quietly, looking bewildered. Then Mike Good came on as Mikey Marine and he ran around the stage shouting and cocking his gun. The wackos applauded loudly again and the silver-haired ladies and gentlemen seemed just as bewildered, although this time a few clapped briefly.

And then it was Val's turn. I wished I'd remembered to bring some antacid tablets with me.

Val stood there for a moment on stage, looking shy and slightly embarrassed. The silver-haired ladies and gentlemen were all smiling at the sight of her beige dress and sensible shoes. But then she began to strip, and they stopped smiling. Some of them gasped. Val stripped down to the black lace nightie. And she picked up a whip. "Tonight Vanna is a bad girl," she said, and she whipped the stage and sang and wriggled and writhed. The audience was silent, and I couldn't tell whether they loved her or hated her. And I wasn't sure how I wanted them to feel. But when she finished, everyone went wild. The wackos rose to their feet, shouting, "Vanna! Vanna! Vanna!" And the silver-haired ladies and gentlemen rose also, yelling, "Bravo! Bravo! Bravissimo!"

After the performance, I went backstage. Val was still wearing the black nightie. She was sitting at her dressing table, surrounded by bouquets of flowers and boxes of chocolates. I was hoping that we could just quietly get back into the car and drive back to Albany. But B. Morrison and Mike Good invited her out to a bar across the street to celebrate. I tagged along. The bar was overpriced and filled with plastic plants and waiters with phony accents, just like the restaurants on Lark Street. I sat between B. Morrison's boyfriend, a banker in a pinstriped suit, and Mike Good's wife, a history professor. They both looked as dazed as I felt. B. Morrison was still wearing Banana Medley's slinky yellow jumpsuit, and Mike Good was in Mikey Marine's combat fatigues. And Val, of course, was in the black nightie. I peeked under the table. Her whip was curled neatly on her lap. They were proposing toasts to each other. "To Mikey!" "To Banana!" "To Vanna!"

Whether I liked it or not, I was sitting there with a bunch of wackos, so I figured I might as well try to make the best of it. I decided to try to make conversation. "So, Mike," I said, "I hear you went to Harvard. What fraternity were you in?"

He looked bewildered. "That's Mike Good you're thinking of. He's just one of my characters. I'm Mikey Marine, fighting machine. I went to war, not college."

What a wacko, I thought, pretending to be his character. I tried again. "Barbara," I pushed my glasses up, "Val tells me your dad's a banker. Which bank, may I ask?"

She looked at me blankly. "I'm Banana Medley and my dad swung from a tree."

Across the table, Val looked at me intensely. She spoke in Vanna's exotic voice. "Oh, Peter," she said, "Vanna thinks the time has come for you to open your eyes and see who it is you're really sitting with!"

And suddenly I knew that what I'd feared most had come true. They weren't pretending. They had each, at last, become their characters. There was no more Barbara Morrison, daughter of bankers. No more Mike Good, Harvard Ph.D. And no more Val, state word processor. I looked at Barbara's boyfriend and at Mike's wife, and I could see that they had just realized it, too. The three of us looked sadly at each other. I sipped my glass of wine and stifled a belch. I'd lost Val. It had been inevitable. Vanna had changed her. My glasses slid down my nose and I didn't even bother pushing them up. I wiped a tear from my eye and saw Barbara's boyfriend and Mike's wife doing the same.

After we'd all had a few drinks, I got into the car with Vanna, and we drove back to Albany together. She was quiet, just staring out the car window and smiling. But this time when I got the urge to make love to her in the car, it was stronger, much stronger, than before. I tried not to stare at her slender calves in the lacy black pantyhose, and I kept waiting for the urge to pass, but it didn't. It kept building and building. It stayed with me the whole way home. And by the time we got to Albany, I couldn't stand it any more. I felt crazed with lust. And it was definitely Vanna I wanted. Vanna in her black nightie and black pantyhose, Vanna with her whip. Not Val with her seersucker pajamas. And when we stepped out of the car, I threw my arms around her. "Oh Peter," she moaned, "Vanna has been waiting."

And we did it on our front lawn, in the moonlight, and it was like nothing I'd ever experienced before. We didn't just kiss and hug, and I didn't just get on top. Vanna leaned over me and she touched me everywhere. She touched parts of my body Val had never touched, parts I'd barely paid attention to myself. She touched and bit and licked and scratched my belly-button, my underarm, the soles of my feet, my hipbones, my collarbone, the insides of my wrists. . . . And then she stood and ran inside the house. "Wait here," she whispered. And I lay there, naked, with the grass tickling me. She returned a minute later holding an egg in each hand, and I thought about the great omelettes that Val sometimes made on Sunday mornings, and I wondered what Vanna was going to do, and then she broke the eggs over my flesh and I was sticky and wet, and, slowly, she licked me completely clean, like a mother cat. And I purred my head off. And then I did it all to her. I touched her all over, and I bit her and licked her and scratched her, and we went back and forth that way, all night long, licking and biting and scratching until the sun rose.

And so, like Barbara Morrison and Mike Good, Val has been taken over by her character. And I'll bet that Laurie Anderson and Eric Bogosian and all the other performance artists out there have all been taken over by their characters, too. To be honest, though, I feel luckier than Barbara's boyfriend and Mike's wife, because I wouldn't want to spend my life with Banana Medley or Mikey Marine. Vanna, remember, can be anyone and everyone. Dominatrix. Virginal child. Harried housewife. Sensitive poet. And so many more. I live with them all. And I love them all. I couldn't be happier. I've opened up, learned to love Vanna in all her guises. My love for Vanna has made me the biggest wacko of all. Vanna and I dance and sing and strip and wriggle and writhe together. And sometimes, for old-time's sake, Vanna becomes a character who wears flowered rayon dresses and is a word processor for the State. She's very sweet, this word processor, and when she's around, we do a lot of kissing and hugging.

ON THE SIDE OF THE ROAD

Margerie stood, throwing up, bending down, on the side of the road. This had been going on for a long time: driving, hardly eating, throwing up, hating the driving. But the alternative—remaining inside the apartment in her town—only occasionally seemed any better. The apartment, when last she'd seen it, had an unopened box of Rice Krispies on the table and a can of Mr. Pibb's in the refrigerator.

She drove. Panicking each time she had to pass yet one more car (checking her blind spot three and four times) or worse, a truck; wincing at sudden, sharp turns. This is my lane, or this is my way, or this is my life, she thought in rhythm with Tanya Tucker on the radio. Lately the winds had been so fierce that she'd felt engaged in a match, as though another pair of hands on the steering wheel were insistently turning in the opposite direction.

One night she drove into a town with three movie theaters and seven bars, and chose, randomly, to enter the fourth bar she came upon. The jukebox was playing a song about a couple very happy in their love until the woman became obsessed with the idea of striking it big in Southern California and left the man back in Tennessee; but, five years later, at the song's conclusion, she's a barmaid in Southern California, while he's living in a mansion in Tennessee.

Margerie sat down at the bar and ordered a Hamm's, wondering if she'd turned out the car lights. What if she hadn't, and the battery ran down, and she had to stay here, in this town, while an unknown mechanic probed and possibly abused parts of her car? She was nauseated immediately, because this was not the town she had chosen to come to, and therefore, she couldn't stay here. Her finger had not landed here; this would merely be absurd.

A man—he was from this town, she guessed, but he might just as well have been plucked from the town she had chosen to live in—sat down beside her at the bar, shifting the weight of his thin, angular body, touching the silver buckle on his leather belt with the finger where the ring usually was. "Cold out there," he said.

"I smell of vomit," she replied. "I've been puking on and off for a few weeks."

He stood up, didn't look back, and walked out of the bar. A few moments later she heard a car start. What if it was her car? What if he had broken in and started it up with a bobby pin, the way the tough boys used to? Once, in the staircase of their building, Tommy Gaglione, his hand beneath her bra, had said, "I took a Mustang clear out to Queens the other night! Queens, man. Doin' 90."

Tommy Gaglione had grown up to become a junkie. One day on the subway she'd spotted him and noted the giveaway sallow skin and decaying teeth, the short-sleeved muscle shirt (exactly the same style, or perhaps exactly the same shirt, from the old days) revealing needle tracks down both arms, lacing onto his hands. Margerie had supposed she ought to feel embarrassed, but she hadn't. She'd been on her way to meet her husband for lunch. Tommy had seen her, too, and grinned in the old way so that she'd know, then nodded out, a contraband cigarette dangling from his lips. She had whispered, almost to him, but not quite to him, as she stood before the opening subway doors, "Your brother didn't . . ." and then she was out the doors, inside the station, heading—with all the others—for an exit. Bills Gaglione, Tommy's brother, had become a cop. Or so Margerie was certain she remembered having heard. Margerie's own brother, who'd been Tommy's friend, had been killed in a wreck when he was nineteen, in a stolen Ford, his body prone and twisted on the highway, though the brown paper bags and tubes of airplane glue remained upright on the back seat.

The advertising man Margerie later married had grown bored, after the first six months, of hearing about the old Brooklyn neighborhood and her family's hardships, her father's business failures and his untimely death; of Margerie's own decision, at seventeen, to free herself from that Brooklyn world with its women in hair rollers, its hold-ups, rapes, beatings, and streetcorner singing groups composed of inarticulate budding gangsters; of how she had then flirted, instead, with the bohemian East Village life: clap and crabs by the time she was eighteen, pot and LSD, mysticism, and an abortion. Just one month, in fact, before Margerie's decision to leave her husband and to come to the town she had chosen, she'd threatened—only slightly not seriously—to murder him with one of their kitchen knives, if he didn't listen one more time to her story of the painful abortion in a New Jersey motel by a doctor without a license who blew his nose and drooled.

She'd first met her husband at a party. He was thirty-three, and she was twenty-three and polished, by then, at being an articulate, vivacious, slightly mysterious hip young girl with a past, impressing him by what he was pleased to label "vampish innocence," and by the abandoned fluency with which she spoke to men of all ages and professions at the party, revealing intimate details of her life in a chatty voice while sipping a constantly refilled glass of bourbon. Even Tommy Gaglione, back in the staircase, had often been forced to mutter, "Shut up!" impatient to get his tongue inside her mouth.

Now, without saying a word—she rarely spoke any longer—Margerie stood up and walked out of the bar, hoping that her car was still in the lot. She had hardly touched her beer; all this time she'd been surviving on Dairy Queen and MacDonald milkshakes, unable even to look at the oozing burgers that the other customers devoured. The chill had fogged up her car's windows with spiderwebs of icy moisture, and Margerie worried that the battery would die, but the car started immediately, and she maneuvered out of the parking lot, back and forth from reverse to drive, without getting stuck on any snow, all of which she felt meant it was time to head back to the apartment in the town she had chosen, two years ago, as the place in which she would live and die. The Interstate was the same whichever direction she drove, and the men still said, "Foxy Beaver," over their CB radios in the southern accents they affected, out here so far from the South, in this part of the country with no distinctive accent and intonation of its own.

Finally she was back at the apartment. Her old and near-deaf neighbor lady had somehow gotten inside her mailbox (probably she'd known the mailman for forty years and had simply said, "Jack, can I have the mail for that quiet lady in number four while she's on her trip?") and had stacked the mail outside Margerie's door, tying it neatly with a pink wool bow. The mail consisted of five letters from her husband.

He had been writing letters for the entire two years, without pause, still attempting, at times, to seduce her back with anecdotes about singing waitresses and rollerskating waiters in new bistros in the West Village, and up-to-date news of his latest accounts; at other times he merely vented his rage. He could not understand that she would stick to this decision, made two years ago on a Sunday, because she had to.

Margerie had gone to visit her mother that Sunday, via the subway into Brooklyn; although her husband wouldn't have viewed a cab ride as an extravagance, she was uncomfortable allowing strange men, seen only as broad backs and half-profiles, to chauffeur her, while the crowded, noisy, sub--terranean IND seemed hardly a vehicle at all. She was carrying a thick cut of steak and a package of sticky buns from a new bakery. For a solid moment, Margerie's mother had peered through the peekhole, before opening the door in her baggy print housedress. They seated themselves side by side at the kitchen table, elbows upon the scrubbed vinyl tablecloth, beneath the two photographs—one of Margerie's father, who had been killed, along with three other passengers, including a fifteen-year-old girl, on a crowded Manhattan bus by a soft-spoken junior high school social studies teacher who declared no memory of the act—and the other, a slightly blurred photograph of Margerie's brother in a torn T- shirt, with lidded eyes, during the James Dean / Marlon Brando days he'd never grown out of. Her mother spoke of a new, tasty low-calorie pudding, of a novel by Joyce Carol Oates she'd taken out of the branch library, of bursitis of the shoulder. As always, the Venetian blinds remained shut, so that the men out on the streets could not take advantage of the view a ground floor apartment might offer.

Tragedies, Margerie's mother believed, were not hers alone: a next-door neighbor had both forehead and neck scarred forever by an eighteen year old with a jagged tin can that had once held chick peas; the Puerto Rican child down the hall had lost an arm while being dangled between subway cars by the fourth cousin everyone had always called El Loco, El Bobo. Margerie's mother proudly called herself a "liberal" if asked, and swore she harbored no resentment against the two dead men who had left her in such a neighborhood (where she was now too settled to leave) supporting herself by secretarial work in her middle years. Margerie left early, afraid to walk to the station in the dark, not staying to share the steak.

Her husband was eating a defrosted blueberry pie and playing "Jeopardy" with their son in the living room, with the TV on. "I'm moving," she announced, before her coat was off. "I'm moving," she repeated, entering the living room, lifting the large atlas from the bookcase, opening to a map of the United States on page twenty-nine, closing her eyes, flinging her finger down, "here."

And he was still writing her letters, after two years. In one letter he'd said, "You have broken all the rules, my dear, and so I see no reason why *I* should follow any. Besides, who would I ask for the etiquette involved? Emily Post? Joyce Brothers?"

Margerie looked around the apartment, then at the five letters and their pink bow, and then walked over to the sink and threw up, scaring a tiny spider. Maybe she should brush her teeth, if there was any toothpaste. On the bathroom floor lay a wrinkled tube of something called "Proud," a new brand from one of the old corporations—one of her husband's most important clients, in fact, if she could remember any longer which were the clients and which were the crucial potential clients.

Afterward, she splashed cold water on her face and lay down on the unmade bed, which was surrounded by two years worth of letters. Flicking the radio switch to On, she heard a voice estimating the number of hogs and cows to be slaughtered in the town's stockyards the next day. She flicked the switch to Off and coughed a thin, pale saliva into an aluminum ashtray, then heaved and shuddered, head hanging over the side of the bed.

One of the newly-arrived letters was ripped, slightly, in the corner, and bore what looked like a catsup stain beside the stamp. She would open that one. The apartment was cold and she buttoned her sweater.

> Margie, I ran into your old friend Laurie, from
> your "group." She wanted me to be sure to tell
> you she's been promoted to a "well-paying mana-
> gerial position" and that your support back in
> those days was a "true and valid" part of her
> learning to become "more assertive."

This was, then, one of the "rational" letters, one of the sarcastic, mocking ones. She read on.

> But Margie, I still miss you in bed. Don't you miss
> me, miss my touch at night, miss the things we
> did? Or are you actually managing to have affairs

out there in that godforsaken crap town in which
you've chosen to rot, for whatever personal,
pathological reasons?

No, it was not a rational one, after all. Perhaps he had
had a drink, or two drinks, between paragraphs. Perhaps he'd
gone out to a cocktail party, perhaps spent the night with a
woman much younger than himself, and returned to the letter, hungover, the following morning. Ignoring the rest of the
letter, she noted, despite herself, the postscript.

P.S. Maybe you no longer exist for me. Maybe
each of these letters is an end in itself.

Margerie dropped the letter onto the floor with all the
others. She needed no sleep, she decided, and stood, draping
her coat across her shoulders, opening the door and walking
to the car, parked across the street. The battery didn't catch,
and then it caught and died. Finally it started, but the back
right tire spun uselessly, until she went outside and placed a
ripped grocery sack beneath it, on top of the ice. There was
a hole on the thumb of her left glove, and the wind hurt the
exposed flesh. The sun was not out yet.

Margerie had driven a full six blocks, had made it to the
dry cleaners and the post office, before needing to pull over.

Standing in front of the post office, ears and nose red-
dened by the wind, waiting for his morning ride to school
or work, was a boy of about nineteen. He approached her.
"Ma'am, are you okay?"

"Pregnant," she lied.

Blushing, he walked back to his place, but he had stepped
in some of her mess, and she saw that it remained, clinging,
to his maroon, pointed cowboy boots. She saw, too, that the
stance and pose he affected were so similar to those of Tommy
Gaglione and Whitey Lenehan and her own brother, although
they hadn't wanted to appear the hardened cowboy-trucker
that this boy did, but as cool, inner-city toughs, untouchable.

She drove with the radio on—she nearly always did—and
sang, tunelessly, along with the woman who wished to go back
to the Blue Bayou to watch the sun rise with her lost lover. The
announcer came on, predicting more snow for the evening,
making a wisecrack about poor old Nellie who would never
be able to see the sun shine again, and Margerie suddenly
remembered one letter from her husband which had arrived
about four months before; one which she'd opened because it
had come in an off-yellow envelope.

> Why *do* you stay out there? What thrill are you
> deriving? I stay awake at night, seriously I do,
> pondering your deviant pleasures. (Incidentally,
> I took your mother out to dinner the other night,
> to an Italian restaurant "without a bar" at her
> request.) Are you spending your days volunteer-
> ing for the local 4-H? Reading Sartre and Camus
> to town geriatrics? Honestly, had you rehearsed
> for weeks with Johnny Carson, you couldn't
> have chosen a more ludicrous town. You once
> said—during the "group" days—that you were
> near to exorcising all the irrational resentments
> and hostilities. And then you go and pull this
> looney tune. Before I forget, I did the campaign
> for the new health cereal, Granette: *you* were the
> big health food nut, not me; thought you'd like
> to know.

To that letter she'd actually mailed back a reply, something she occasionally did, because she did not think she hated
her husband in any way at all. She assumed he was doing an
adequate job of raising Philip: making certain that he didn't
ride his bike in the park along any but the most populated
paths, that the private school he attended emphasized both
creative and pragmatic learning, that Father and Son still met
for their weekly lunches in the Kozy Kitchen. Her letter had
been brief.

I stay only because I need to pare things down.
There is no pleasure involved. There never has
been.

He'd replied in a thick red ink with ferocious blots and
loops.

Oh, so now you fancy yourself a pear? Well, you
just come on back to the big apple and I'll sink
my sharp teeth into your juicy skin. Let me have
one more bite, my lawful wedded fruitcake, my
pear lady, and I'll teach you the pleasures of fruit
punch, jello mold, and fruit cocktail.

On the day she'd received that letter, she'd driven
through three towns, pulling over to the side of the road at
twenty-minute intervals, seeing bits of pear, undigested, floating in the bilious liquid, at each stop.

And now, months later, Margerie found herself pulling
into a bar in one of those same towns. Left hand in her pocket
to avoid the wind, she carefully stepped through the icy parking lot, past the few cars and one van already parked. Inside,
standing at the bar and ordering another Hamm's, she felt ill
almost immediately. "Not too many *ladies* come in here," the
bartender joked by rote, answering her question and pointing
his finger in the general direction.

At the juke box, her way was blocked by a woman with
teased blonde hair, wearing a tight white jersey turtleneck,
tight black skirt, and 1955-style Bunny Hug black shoes, bending over the machine, reading song titles. The woman sniffed
and looked up. "Hey, what have *you* been doing?"

Margerie felt sicker than before. The woman had spoken
in a voice which might have been Tommy Gaglione's sister's.

"I'd like to get by to wash. I don't feel . . ."

The woman straightened herself. "Come on up to my
room. This filthy outhouse won't get you no cleaner—yeah,
there are rooms upstairs—not to mention that certain sights
and odors will make you sicker."

Margerie followed the blonde woman up narrow stairs to a dusty second floor, and inside to her room, in which there was a poster on one wall that read, "Scorpio . . . Cancer," above a drawing of a nude male and female embracing, and another that read, 'Keep On Truckin.' " Margerie splashed cold water on her face, then placed her head beneath the faucet, so that her long hair was separated into disagreeable, clinging strands down her neck and onto her shoulders.

The blonde woman sat on the bed, watching. "You're from the city."

Margerie nodded.

"I'm from the Bronx," the woman grinned, "around where Dion came from. But there's one thing I want to get straight, and that is that I'm not getting into some kind of friend-thing with you. I don't even like women very much, generally. I drink with men. I party with men. Nine years ago I followed my ex-husband out here, because I was one of those suckers who married for *love*. What I'm saying is that you and I aren't going to be girlfriends."

Margerie spotted, for the first time, the now-faded tracks along the woman's arms: "I hadn't thought so." Obviously they were old, though, from the days of Dion and the Belmonts and her ex-husband. There was also a prominent, fresh bruise. The water ran and Margerie stood, foolishly, until the blonde woman walked to the sink and turned off the faucet. "Okay, baby," she laughed, "you're as clean as you're going to be until you get home."

Downstairs, the woman stopped before the jukebox again. "Help me pick out a song. Should I play one about how helpless she feels loving a no-good man, or one about screw you, buddy, Mama didn't raise me to live with a bum like you."

"It doesn't matter." Margerie feared she might throw up again. "Any. None."

The woman laughed slightly. "Press E-13." Margerie's fingers shook.

The blonde woman leaned against the Wurlitzer sign. "Okay. Catch you later."

And Margerie heard her brother affectionately calling out
to his kid sister as he left the house for one of his adventures:
"Take it light, bimbo. Catch you later, bitch . . . "

Margerie left the bar and began to drive, skidding sharp-
ly at the very first turn she had to make. She wondered, a few
minutes later, as she waited for a traffic light to change, if she
should reply to her husband's last letter. The next town had a
lit-up Dairy Queen, and she ordered a vanilla shake. Inside her
car, in the parking lot, she sat, sipping and writing, her pen
mimicking the rhythm of the announcer's voice on the radio,
warning motorists of extremely hazardous road conditions.

> You ask why I'm here, you imply that there is
> something unconscious driving me. You use the
> word "pathology." Yes. Something with no name
> at all. If you can think of a label for it, I'm sure
> you'll copyright it, find the perfect designer and
> the most fetching TV model. You'll celebrate
> with whiskey sours. But until you name it, it is
> all mine.

Slowly driving back to her apartment, back to the town
she had chosen, she mailed the letter en route, dropping it
into the snow-covered slot of a mailbox on the side of the
road. Much later that night she lay in bed, listening to winds
raging and howling, which she was nearly convinced were not
winds at all, but hundreds of car engines being revved-up and
stopped, starting and dying, all night long.

THE FLOWERS

Flower and maiden were different and
yet the same . . .
—Nathaniel Hawthorne

Blonde Rhoda from Ponka, Nebraska, dreams that a flower eats her younger sister Elaine. Blonde Elaine stands, smiling dreamily, before a slender-stemmed, pink tulip, when suddenly the tulip's petals open wide, revealing a mouth: Elaine is snapped up quickly, neatly swallowed and consumed, whole. Rhoda doesn't fully wake up from the dream. She doesn't need to; the dream is planted, firmly, in her memory.

In Guayaquil, Ecuador, a young boy, Enrique, is walking along a path. He is thirteen years old and has already had sex twice, both times with the daughter of his neighbor's maid. He swaggers his tiny butt, he struts, he sways; he reminds himself that he, alone of all his friends, has had sexual relations. Then, without warning, a heavy-branched black tree uproots itself from the side of the path, and begins to take mincing steps

97

toward him. It stands directly in his way, swoops down, and devours him. He is sure that this has really happened, and yet somehow he is able to continue walking into town, there to do an errand for his mother.

Years later, Enrique's family moves from Ecuador to New York City. His father, wealthy back in Ecuador, has lost most of the family's money through poor investments. Humiliated, the family moves to a Manhattan ghetto to be near richer relatives. Enrique takes evening courses at the City College of New York; his ambition is to become a successful photographer of beautiful women and landscapes.

Blonde Rhoda from Ponka, Nebraska, has also moved to New York City. First she leaves Ponka to attend college in Minneapolis. Then she follows her college boyfriend to New York. A year later, they break up and she moves with her two turtles into a studio apartment. She finds a job as an administrative assistant in a midtown bank, and discovers that she loves the single life.

Elaine, Rhoda's blonde younger sister, the victim of a tragic car crash a few years before, is back home in Ponka, permanently crippled from the waist down. She remains at home in a wheelchair, only occasionally allowing herself to feel embittered; mostly she endeavors to be kind and cheerful. Her parents take care of her. She faithfully writes one long letter to Rhoda every single day.

Rhoda has grown up to be beautiful: her blonde hair is cut short and shaggy, flattering to her enormous green eyes. Her turtlenecks, tight skirts, and high leather boots make her a great favorite at the bank. Coincidentally, also a favorite at the bank is Olga, Enrique's twenty-four-year-old sister, who works as a teller there. Olga goes out of her way to win favor with the blonde, higher-paid Rhoda. Although Rhoda attended college and Olga did not, their interests are much the same: they love to dance and they love to sip elegant-sounding drinks. Crème de menthe is a special treat. They also love to read novels with powerful and happy endings. Olga is fascinated by her fair Midwestern friend; Rhoda is intrigued by the red- lipsticked, black-haired South American woman. They agree not to be jealous of each other because they are such different types that surely the same man would never be attracted to both of them.

At home, Enrique has begun writing poems. Plants of all sorts recur in his work.

> The yellow tree is wide
> It is yawning
> It is gaping
> It
>   swallows
>   us.

One day Olga takes Rhoda home to visit her family. The family has been excited for a week, awaiting the visit of Olga's friend. Olga has raved on and on about Rhoda, telling them that she looks much like Farrah Fawcett, the movie actress. Rhoda and Olga catch a bus heading uptown after work; a steaming dinner, prepared by Olga's mother, awaits them.

Olga is especially pleased at how well Rhoda looks that day, in her yellow cotton pantsuit and yellow wedge espadrilles. She carries a large purple canvas pocketbook, and Olga is delighted at the daring way her friend mixes and matches colors.

Enrique arrives just a few minutes after the women. By day, he tutors in a community storefront, plays soccer, and smokes pot; then, stoned, he rushes in for dinner and then off to his classes at City College. But today he has decided to skip his class, so that he can spend time getting to know his sister's friend. All week long, his family has teased him. His father said, "Enrique will fall in love with this blonde friend of Olgita's. You will see!" His teenaged brother laughed, "A blonde? Nice legs? You're a goner!" Two days before Rhoda's visit, Enrique writes this poem:

> Yellow winged
> bees, green thick leaves,
> Yellow bees green leaves
> In love in love in love . . .

Dinner is rice with black beans, fried bananas, thick, rich slices of meat with red sauce. Enrique's mother (newly a tyrant, since the move to New York City) says, "Enrique . . . you will tell Olga's pretty friend of your vision . . ." Enrique blushes. He swallows some meat. It's not a real blush; he has intuited already that Rhoda has fallen under the spell of his proud good looks, and he is merely pretending modesty. "Enrique, yes, yes, tell!" Olga cries. She adores her brother.

Rhoda, meanwhile, is delighting in the meal, the black beans, especially. Only once before has she eaten such beans, in a Brazilian restaurant with a man in the import-export business who did not call for a second date.

Enrique begins. "I was thirteen, we still lived in Guayaquil then. And I was walking along, alone . . . you see, I was already quite mature, developed much more so than other boys . . ."

(He deliberately stares—for an instant—at Rhoda's breasts.)

"And I was walking along on a road, but not a road like in New York, not like Broadway, for example . . . barely a path, newly carved, dusty, with much vegetable life, with tall, tall grass and trees, and suddenly . . ."

(He pauses, swallows a sip of beer. Oh, he relishes, savors, this part in the telling . . . he notes Rhoda's green eyes upon him, her anticipatory smile.)

"A tall, angry tree . . . a black tree . . . a monster tree of some sort! . . . moved away from its position on the side of the path . . . do you understand what I'm saying? *A tree walked!*"

(Rhoda smiles brightly.)

"*A tree walked*—a maddened, living thing it was—and it stood before me and bent down. It bent with grace, like a dancer . . . and its branches touched the tip of my head . . . I was not tall for my age. . . ."

(He includes this detail to show the honesty of his narrative; no embellished fabrication is this!)

"And it had a mouth somewhere . . . a hole, a large, gaping hole . . . and it came for me, and it swallowed me alive. . . . And I lived within that tree for a long time after that. Though I also lived in the real world, I lived there, as well. . . . I saw many things."

(He pauses, looks down, the false blush returning.)

Now Olga explains: "Enrique didn't really live in the tree. At least not within the dimensions we know in our world . . . but you must understand that my family and our friends . . . we do believe that Enrique did have this experience in some other dimension or spiritual realm. We believe that he is mystically blessed, and we honor him for this."

(Olga hopes that Rhoda and Enrique will fall in love. This is why she has brought Rhoda home for dinner in the first place. If Rhoda becomes her sister-in-law, they will always stay best friends! Shyly, she stares at Rhoda.)

But Rhoda is weeping. Tears are streaming, pouring, cascading down her face. "My crippled sister Elaine," she sobs, "was devoured by a tulip! I always knew it wasn't just a dream, that I'd been allowed a glimpse of something far more important! Always, ever since that night, a look in Elaine's eyes told me she was somewhere else, but I never put the two things together! Until now. . . ."

Olga stands up. She holds her glass of 7-Up high above her head. "A toast!" she shouts. "A toast for my brother Enrique, who is mystically blessed, and a toast to Rhoda, my best girlfriend, also mystically blessed! I believe in this, in magic, in love . . . I'll do a Tarot reading. . . ." She rushes from the room to get her cards.

The table is cleared. Enrique sits up straight, a gleam of pure joy in his eyes. Olga arranges the cards. Rhoda chooses cards from the deck, which Olga then reads. "This means," declares Olga, concentrating hard, "that your vision was beautiful and real, and that you were meant to fall in love on this night." She reshuffles the deck so that Enrique may then choose his cards, and Olga reads once more. Her happiness is superb. "The cards show us everything!" she shouts with joy. "You too, my brother, were meant to fall in love tonight! You were meant to fall in love with your spiritual equal, with my girlfriend Rhoda!"

"Oh no! No! Not with me," gasps Rhoda. "You must love and marry my sister Elaine, back in Ponka. She's the one who was blessed and meant for you, not me!"

The room falls silent. Then Enrique's mother nods her consent; his father slowly does the same. Olga clenches her fists tightly, so that she will not speak out. Enrique is at first blank, but then he nods, as well. Yes, he will live with Elaine in Ponka, Nebraska; he hopes that she is an excellent cook, a benevolent person, that she keeps a nice garden in the backyard. Enrique meets Rhoda's eyes and smiles to assure her that he will do what he is destined to do. He will love Elaine. He closes his eyes, and suddenly, Elaine, herself, is before him, with her blonde hair tied back by a shining pink ribbon, her skin just a shade paler than her sister's. She beckons to him. "My love," she calls gently from her seated position. "Oh, my love . . ." Now, even if he never again has another vision, his life will be much more than complete.

Rhoda curls up in her chair, folding her slender arms around herself. At last, after so long, she has found peace.

SHANA. SANDY.
BRENDA. LORRAINE.

Shana with whom I was supposedly eternally, intimately bound, after we pricked our pinkies one rainy Saturday
with a needle from her mother's sewing kit, although we were
in tenth grade and too old for such superstition.

Sandy who could always secure money from somewhere
(her parents? a piggy bank?) to lend me when I needed it for
shoes with an open teardrop design, or a silver pendant with
a turquoise stone to match my turquoise sweater.

Brenda who first talked openly about sexual longings, in-
spiring me to share my own longings in a way I haven't allowed
myself since, not even with my husband, although there are
moments when I know for the marriage's sake, I should.

And Lorraine, so timid that when Mr. Rodriguez, the
Spanish teacher, forgot to call her name during attendance

for an entire week, she wept silently in the back of the room.

Shana now . . . married once, divorced once, married again, a mother of one per marriage, and happy the second time around, with a big home in the suburbs and two cars. Season's Greetings cards to me are sent on time, signed, "Fondly, Shana, Roger, Jessica, and Presley!"

Sandy, academic and intellectual, finishing a Ph.D. at a "very prestigious school"—this in a P.S. in one of Shana's Season's Greetings cards; she'd heard this "from somewhere," it said.

Brenda. Drugs. Living out West. In a house filled with others who dropped out, well over a decade ago, when it seemed the thing to do.

And Lorraine I heard about by accident, through a cousin of hers met coincidentally in the drapery section of a department store, who informed me in hushed tones that, "Oh, Lorraine? She's . . ." then she sized me up, decided, I suppose, why not, ". . . just had another breakdown, this time for real . . ." and then looked at me almost angrily, as though if only I had cared enough way back then, things might have been different today.

Shana. Sandy. Brenda. Lorraine.

Then college years, and

Barbara. Lois. Cathy.

In Anthropology 101, puberty rites and Margaret Mead. In Psychology 101, were we oral personalities, did our boyfriends have unresolved Oedipal complexes?

Discussing, in the Rathskeller, women professors who let their hair grey naturally, so much more aesthetic than our mothers, and male professors who jogged and were thin and bearded, not like our fathers, chubby and worried.

Discussing, until three a.m., with Lois and her boyfriend Nick, my inability to ever, ever complete a paper on time.

"Did your parents punish you for lateness as a child?" asked Nick.

"Are you afraid of success?" asked Lois, holding Nick's hand.

Barbara was my roommate then, and Lois lived down the hall, and Cathy lived with Lois, and we were inseparable.

Barbara. Lois. Cathy.

Barbara and I finally came to a parting of the ways over my not keeping the room neat and clean, though she asked nicely and I continually agreed, yes, I knew which chores were mine, and really, I did know.

Lois and I came to a parting of the ways when I went on a date behind her back with Nick, since he'd asked me when she was off on a ski trip, and I hadn't learned yet how to say no to men.

And Cathy went crazy our senior year, talking about "voices" and "leaders" and the "work" she alone, in a world gone mad, could do. She would find others like herself, she swore. Her mother wrote a letter to each of us, asking what signals we had seen, and each of us wrote back that honestly, we'd seen none.

Barbara. Lois. Cathy.
And never can I leave out Dixie.

Dixie.

Diane, though we called her Dixie because of all the ice cream in cups she devoured daily; nobody existed but mommy, daddy, brother, sister, and Dixie, my first best friend. But Dixie moved away when she was nine, one August morning in a U-Haul, her mother and stepfather kissing me goodbye and calling me "darling."

A few years ago, while riding a bus, I thought I saw her, walking a fluffy, dog, wearing a white dress, gorgeous, sophisticated; it was probably someone else, though, some other gorgeous, sophisticated woman whose name was Dorothy but as a child was called Didi. The woman turned the corner too quickly as the light changed.

No class reunions have brought any of us together. No terribly dramatic meetings, no twists of fate: not in the women's room in O'Hare airport, not at a hotel bar in Mexico City. Lois and I have not tearfully allowed bygones to be bygones in the waiting room of a gynecologist's office, Cathy hasn't tiptoed up to me in the library, admitting that yes, she'd really been bizarre back then in college, but is so much better now.

Even my dreams don't allow much: Brenda and I meet beneath a green sea, but we are swimming opposite ways underwater in a sea world that is filled with fish in the shapes of sharp knives.

Sometimes I just repeat their names over and over, for no reason, the same way I half-sing, half-speak, the words of popular songs.

My husband and I have no children, and so there's no opportunity to watch my daughter playing with other little girls, with

Jennifer. Caroline. Nicole. Celeste.

Instead, I have many opportunities to sip wine at dinner and wonder whether Dixie somehow, somewhere, met up with Cathy and joined her cult, and whether I am number one hundred and one on Shana's Season's Greetings card list. Does her husband, Roger, say yearly, "Why do you even bother sending cards to her anymore?" Does she nod, acknowledging the silliness of licking the envelope, of affixing the stamp, too much a creature of habit, or of something else, to stop?

My husband asks me why Shana still sends me cards, after all, when I haven't responded in years.

My husband asks me why, whenever we travel, I find the local telephone directory and look up all their names.

"Half of them are probably married, anyway," he says, "and use different last names."

"What would you do," he says, "if you found out that Dixie *is* living in Bennington?"

My husband asks me why, if I'm really so interested in all my old friends, I don't just locate their families and ask.

Why, my husband wonders, since I do know where Shana is, at least, don't I try to rekindle that friendship and see if there's still anything.

He suspects that a smugness of some sort motivates me, that I believe in special female bonds, girlhood secrets and understandings to which I long to return; he thinks I'm trying to tell him that our marriage hasn't been enough for me.

"You're wrong," I finally tell him, one evening in a motel room in Brookings, South Dakota, where he has just had an unsuccessful interview for a teaching position, while I thumb through the Brookings telephone directory. "It's that I'm mad at all of them." He seems not to have heard. "I'm angry," I repeat.

He, of course, has his own anger at the moment: anger at me for what he perceives as my lack of interest, anger at a dean who made it clear that he would really prefer to hire a woman, anger at the bleakness of the motel room, anger at the winter storm outside.

His anger is nothing compared to mine. And he'll never know how angry I am, because that is the secret that I keep inside. It's better that way. I'll never tell him how I hold onto my anger, how I nurture it and keep it alive, how it angers me still, that Barbara cared more about having a neat, dust-free college room than she ever did about me.

And that Sandy, so smug and proud about having gotten her Ph.D. in some obscure field, writing her scholarly papers that nobody will ever read, never thinks to send me a card or a note.

And that when Mr. Rodriguez forgot to call Lorraine's name in Spanish class, it was I who went up to him quietly to tell him of his error, and now Lorraine is off somewhere breaking down, not thinking of me at all, not thinking about how we played with dolls even when we were too old, not thinking of me at all, and hasn't in years.

Shana. Sandy. Brenda. Lorraine.
Barbara. Lois. Cathy.
Dixie.

None really cared enough, ever really wanted to know me fully, to love me forever, and of course, if I said all this to my husband, he would look at me with that expression he gets and tell me that it sounds to him as though there are problems deeper than I care to admit, and of course, that's exactly what I don't wish to hear my husband say to me, and so I remain, in the motel in Brookings, South Dakota, holding the phone directory in my lap, counting the minutes until he will fall asleep.

THE STAR-CROSSED LOVE OF DON DIEGO DEL PERRO AND CHASTITY

A Solemn Exchange
Of Poetic Vows,
Across An Ocean,
Between Don Diego del Perro and Chastity

I, Don Diego del Perro,
Pledge fidelity to the woman, Chastity, abroad.
That woman of strange moods. Accidentally
Sticking her foot in the mouths of others.
Paint splatters around her; eight-ounce tumblers crack;
Oven cleaners molest her palms;
Electric fans yearn to bite; electric blenders

Wish the whipping of her flesh.
Still, I pledge undying love,
In the male fashion
Of our era.

I, Chastity,
Abroad in this land of midgets and churches,
Think of thee drinking vile liquids,
Eyeing the bodies of street gals beneath thee,
Eyeing ladies in shawls, too; writing songs,
Tearing them to angry bits; flinging thy guitar about;
Then, with a flourish,
A grocery list impeccably.
I pledge everlasting affection, though
I wear rouge in the evenings, answer knocks
Upon my door.

Letters Between Don Diego del Perro and Chastity
The First Year Apart

Dear C.,
A kitten desecrated my latest song. I am angry.
The old elixers no longer work. I am seeking new ones.
You always sound so happy in your letters.

Dearest Don Diego del Perro, sweet mynah,
Yesterday I dreamed you threw lye in the face of a young
       girl child.

Letters Between Don Diego del Perro and Chastity
The Second Year Apart

Dear C.,
A swarthy stranger passed through last month,
Saying you wear only dark colors,
That midgets light your cigarettes.

Dearest Don Diego del Perro, agitated chipmunk,
I dream of women in green aprons,
Tossing salads, stroking grapes, impaling apples.

> *Letters Between Don Diego del Perro*
> *and Chastity*
> *The Third Year Apart*

Dear C.,
A dark traveler said you bake and broil meat for the midgets,
That you fall down stairs, prefer indigo stew to all others.

Dearest Don Diego del Perro, helpless goat,
I dream you carry a knife, smile overtly, take
liberties.

> *Letters Between Don Diego del Perro*
> *and Chastity*
> *The Fourth Year Apart*

Dear C.,
Is it true you now set pot holders afire?
Use brooms where mops are required?
Dearest Don Diego del Perro, sullen squirrel,
Your guitar is newly painted; You dance all night with the
woman who smuggles cocaine.

> *Letters Between Don Diego del Perro and Chastity*
> *The Fifth Year Apart*

Dear C.,
Whose songs do you wail off-key at odd hours?
Why are you familiar with crimson birds?

Dearest Don Diego del Perro, mad buzzard,
I beg for my sight back; crones cackle in reply.

> *Letters Between Don Diego del Perro and Chastity*
> *The Sixth Year Apart*

Dear C.,
I wandered the graveyard for six days.
I was sad. I wrote many songs.
You would not like these songs.

Dearest Don Diego del Perro, fertile troll,
I woke up at once. A midget crawled from my clock.
I could not enter church.

After the Reconciliation
With Her Lover Don Diego del Perro,
Chastity Confides in her Favorite Girlfriend
While Lunching in a Delicatessen

Oh, did I tell you I tried all kinds of things to make
the evenings pass more quickly? Herbs in my hair, yogurt
six times daily, mantras at midnight, contributing weekly to
the recycling center, refusing hamburgers and steaks? Did I
tell you I read novels? Sometimes poetry?

It was so hard, the midgets kept coming to my door, asking for kisses. I would beg them to kiss my neighbors, to kiss
the shopkeepers, the saloon girls. But it was always me they
wanted to kiss, my lips meant something, do you know what
I mean?

I don't like this cole slaw, not tart enough, don't you
agree? You can have mine if you want. We had no cole slaw
abroad, no, no pastrami, no spare ribs, either.

I surrounded my bed with Don Diego's songs, I sang
all evening, in bed, in the bath. I recited his name. I spent
hours at the stove hoping to recapture my Granny's sauces
and soups. The midgets were such darlings, scouring everywhere for thyme and chile and other things. I burned with
jealousy over long-limbed blondes in pleasant blouses, baking
bread. Do you know the type?

The mailman in the village thought me mad because of
all the snakes in brown wrappers arriving, postage due. The
snakes nibbled the leaves of my plants; green insects attacked
their eyes. I fell down a flight of stairs and couldn't walk for

six months, and oh, how those midgets took advantage of me then; certainly I couldn't attend church, because I couldn't walk! My mother wrote to tell me she'd meant to name me Scarlett Jezebel, but the deaf nurse on duty had misread my father's lips.

I burned a mutt in effigy, later to discover that Don Diego was struck by a migraine at the precise moment the tail went up in flames. I recruited the crazy midget Bobo to bring me goat's hair, which I stuffed in an old sheet twisted in Don Diego's likeness, while Bobo danced on top of my chest of drawers and sang.

Shall we have coffee? I shall take mine black. I was blind for six months and couldn't read his letters. The blacksmith's wife refused to read them aloud to me, declaring certain things better left unspoken, and went to cleanse her hands in the river. Bobo burned the letters. When my sight returned, I salvaged merely one charred "S." Sometimes I'd awaken with purple bruises, round circles of lavendar and maroon. Many weeks I couldn't speak at all. At times I'd have voice only for the natives' tongue. On the very worst days, I'd know only the midget's dialect. If I tried to say Don Diego's name aloud—in any language—I'd choke.

Meanwhile, of course, there were the endless parties. Oh yes, it's a social, gay life there in the village. We'd meet Sundays at the altar, then we'd picnic in the afternoon, eating the most luscious fruits (fruit you couldn't imagine!) and then we'd dance and dance all evening long.

There was this one tall, dark man in town—but I shouldn't talk about him now—what's the point? Don Diego was never out of my mind, even when . . . well, I promised this man certain things, but it wasn't what you think . . . you could say we had an understanding in a way . . . and I am a bit nervous about leaving so suddenly the way I did . . . he seemed a bit vengeful, very *macho*, if you know what I mean. . . . I learned to dress a different way, have you noticed? My necklaces and earrings, have you seen? How much shinier my hair is? How much redder my cheeks are, my skin so smooth?

Still, I never learned to work the Xerox machine abroad,

or how to adjust the TV; my radio was all static; the drains in my sink clogged; pilot lights on the stove never stayed lit; aluminum pans burned while I slept; my telephone set off sparks, and the line be- came crossed with women who whispered all night long.

Are you through with the coffee? How much tip shall we leave? Let's not walk along the side streets, too many crazy men, grabbing, begging. Don Diego is waiting for me uptown in a theater, with buttered popcorn.

Don Diego del Perro Begins to Vacillate While Watching a Televised Baseball Game And Drinking Dark Beer At the Home of a Good Buddy

I don't know. Yeah, I still like her. I don't know. Go! Go! Stupid . . . I'm not sure what I want anymore. Damn! Damn! Did you see that?

Well, I like her, still, a lot. I think she knows, yeah, I think she knows there have been others. She's got to know I'm only human, a healthy male, you know . . .

It's been six years, though, for God's sake. I've written so many new songs, none of which are to her. She broke my stereo yesterday, spilled a vodka sour on the white rug, made a long-distance call for an hour on my phone before realizing it was the wrong party. My beard gives her bad dreams; her new jewelry is ugly as hell; her birds squawk all night long.

Damn! Did you see that play? Why do they send someone like him out? Damn! Hand me another . . . it just isn't the same anymore. I don't know. Who cares?

Bobo the Midget has a Vision

I see her in a soiled, torn white dress. On a mountain top. A man with bushy hair, a beard, a bearish man, is beside her. Is a dog howling? Chastity is crying. The man's lips are parted. What does this mean? Is that man Don Diego? Someone else?

Why is she wearing stained white? Why atop a mountain? I'll go mad! I must know!

I took an egg white, threw it into a clear, sparkling glass, and awaited this vision for hours. But the vision speaks not at all, much like Chastity's television set of hazy pictures and no words.

Yes, I admit that Chastity adored teaching the midgets, but I was special, I must have been. For it was in me alone (only me!) that she confided her love for Don Diego del Perro. It was me she trusted to keep watch for the tall, dark man of our town, allowing her time to hide Don Diego's songs and photographs. Only I knew (me, little Bobo, the one everyone calls crazy!) what the snakes were for; our mailman is such an innocent, a dolt, really. For me alone she performed the double-jointed stunts she'd once won prizes for.

I must see Chastity again! She must return! Perhaps she'll miss me, or the climate of our land; perhaps she'll crave the doting attention of the midgets, perhaps even the bleating of our goats.

Ah, Chastity, I fear for you. Don Diego is a man engrossed in his songs, his guitar, baseball, bars. I will send glossy postcards of the town to you, a lock of my hair, the skin of your favorite snake. I will write songs to you, songs better than his!

But why atop a mountain? Should I have used the yolk instead of the white? Hard-boiled it? Is she climbing toward something? Running away? Is one of them hoping to push the other off?

Why did she leave us now? Ah Chastity, our lost and double-jointed sweet!

Chastity's Favorite Girlfriend Confides,
About Chastity, to Another Girlfriend,
While Lunching in a Greek Coffee Shop

. . . don't know what to do with her. I'm completely empathetic . . . I know what it's like to lose a boyfriend you really care about while you're being pursued by some guy you don't care that much about, but who's making super enticing offers. God, does she confide in me. All night long. She takes the crosstown bus over, wearing funny ripped dresses and icky jewelry, plops down on my living room rug (this is annoying my roommate no end, I'll tell you) and goes on and on and on about Don Diego del Perro. Oh, he doesn't feel the same, six years was too long for him, she can't understand why! Sometimes I doubt her sanity, I don't know what happened to her abroad. Maybe the food, or the sermons, or dancing with too many midgets . . .

Plus, she's stopped answering her doorbell and reading her mail, because she's convinced that this tall dark guy from over there is after her. I keep telling her to talk to this guy, to simply pick up the phone and talk to him, un- less he's a sociopath or something, how can it hurt, right? I mean, she's not sixteen years old, she must know how to say, "Look, I really like you, but only as a friend."

One scary thing is, the post office is suing her because all these snakes, postage due, keep arriving in the mail, and she won't claim them. Can you imagine? Her skin is paler, blue and purple circles under her eyes. Sometimes I'll be downtown shopping and there she'll be, just walking back and forth. Panhandlers ignore her. I call her name, she doesn't even blink. Once I ran over to her and shook her. Nothing. Well, I'm four feet eleven, but I can pack a punch if I have to. So I punched her in the stomach. Nothing! She sort of brushes at me and keeps going. I'm getting worried.

I've told her—I don't know how many times—to see a therapist. I've given her the names of a good Sullivanian and a good feminist Gestalt. She gets this spooky look in her eyes and laughs this spooky laugh. "I'm beyond therapy," she says, "way beyond."

Anyway, Chastity complains of back pains, stomach pains, muscle spasms, shortness of breath, dryness in her mouth. "I'm beyond doctors," she says.

I even called Don Diego del Perro! I figured maybe he could do something, anything! And I hardly even know the guy. He says, "I *thought* that was Chastity wandering around downtown the other day, but I couldn't believe it, her eyes . . ." Then he begins to cry a little bit over the phone; you know the way men do when they're trying to show they have feelings? Then he hiccups and gasps for a full minute. "I'm sorry," he says, "but six years was too long, and she got friendly with all those midgets. I'd still go to films with her, restaurants, you know." I remind him he promised her certain things. He cries and hiccups again and says he has to go to a baseball game with someone named Mara.

I'm honestly nervous about Chastity. Really, she used to be fun. The last time I saw her, she was sprawled on my sofa, complaining of a fever. Anyway, my roommate stuck a thermometer in her mouth, and sure enough, *one hundred and six!* And guess what! We put her to bed, figuring we'd call a doctor in the morning, and in the morning Chastity is gone! Could you just die? And since she won't respond to the phone or the doorbell or the mail, how can I find her?

The Soliloquy of Don Diego del Perro
at Chastity's Death Bed

Oh, Chastity, I never said enough. The doctors tell me it's a rare thing you've caught, unique to women, particularly to women who have traveled abroad and lived elsewhere. Blisters, swellings, blind eyes, your body twisted up so! "Oh, my legs!" you cry. "I am strangled," you moan. Chastity, who do you call a rogue? To whom do you apologize? Why do you ask for mercy? No, no dogs are attacking you, my dearest.

Chastity, why do you suddenly strike out at me like that? Doctor, she suddenly attacked me. . . . Chastity, the doctor wants to see you alone now, he says he has medicine to make these last moments less painful. She refuses to see you, Doctor, she says she'll spit blood in your face and turn your daughter paranoid, your wife anorexic.

Oh, Chastity, I didn't care that much about the mangled stereo, the stains on my sofa, not really. The women in the streets, the women at the ballet, the women who knit me gloves . . . diversions. It had been so long—two thousand, one hundred and ninety days—you must understand! And your letters always sounded happy!

Who are all these elderly women you've recently befriended? And the girls with olive skins, with scarves around their necks? My buddy spotted you at the circus; he said you were flushed. Chastity, why do you telephone at six in the morning, only to have coughing fits over the line? And why do you tell me your dreams in languages I don't understand!

I'm sorry you spent months in bed, unable to walk, writhing. But rumor has it you weren't always alone; some talk about a tall, dark man; I confess that I, too, dream, Chastity! I wish you could have sung my songs in tune, on key, but you don't care about melody, and you define harmony incorrectly! The foods you prepared were inedible: clumps of uncooked things floating in soup, Chastity; hairy things in the stews. And your dolls, the dolls! Did you seriously believe for one moment that we could have made a proper home together, with such motley creatures: baby dolls with black booties, wax dolls with cows' heads, rag dolls, puppets with scowls?

Chastity, last week I did want to kiss you, but you sat in the train station with some dirty old crone, playing with crayons, drawing circles on the benches in the waiting room.

The doctor signals that we haven't much time together; your hospital gown is growing looser moment by moment; you shrink with pain and contortions. Why do you stick your tongue out? In defiance or agony? But wait! You speak! You ask that I plunge a knife into your breast, darling, but it's silly, you're dying anyway. You beg me to take hold of this silver dagger—Chastity, this is simply gauche, having a silver dagger beside your bed; you've read too many novels—but I will if you want me to, because I have denied you so much. And I do, Chastity, I do plunge this dagger into your flesh and watch as you fade—Chastity, you fade!—there is nothing, nothing at all on your bed, this is not death, there is no corpse, no ashes, no guts, no heart, there is nothing, no sign of that loyal body. Ah, this germ unique to women who have lived elsewhere has erased you! If I take the dagger to my own breast, I will only bleed, like any mortal man, I will bleed onto the hospital floor, and I do, I do plunge it into my own skin, and I die in this ugly manner, limbs flailing, there is no music in my death. I was not the prince, after all, was I, Chastity?

FLUENT

Affluent: That's the best word to describe my upbringing; how that word has affected me to this day! One word sums up a lifetime: not at all an unattractive word, wouldn't you agree? Sometime soon you'll have to tell me all about your own upbringing, about how your parents spoke to you, how your brothers and sisters treated you, about the schools you attended. . . . It's important, if we're really going to go through with what we began last week—and it certainly looks as though we are, for here you sit, drink in hand, a second time, with your eyes even darker than last time—that I know about such things. You don't need to worry: nothing you will say could turn me away; this step is being taken after three years of marriage, and I understand what I'm doing, what risks I'm taking; the consequences are clear.

Dominick is away for a few days, don't ask where, don't ask about his business or his professional lifestyle. . . .

If you're going to spend the night this time . . . please do, I want you to . . . then it's urgent that I tell you about nighttime. That's what all this is leading up to. You look so bewildered, so anxious . . . the expressions on your face change so often . . . but I don't want to allow myself to be distracted now.

We weren't la crème de la crème, nowhere near the wealthiest, by any means. My sense of who we are is not at all inflated, rather realistic, I think. "Well-off," my soft-spoken father would say. "Quite well-to-do," my mother said just once in my presence to a distant cousin of hers from Arizona whom, I suppose, had asked. My father provided well; he was one of a long line of men who had done so and who had left him the ways and means to do so easily, as well; and he met their every expectation. And he did so happily, without questions or regrets.

There were only the three of us, two adults and myself. I never wanted for anything. •

Never wanted: Two more crucial words, leading up to what happens to me each evening. It is impossible for me— rationally, during daylight, that is—to believe that I shall ever, ever genuinely want for anything. It's true, dire predictions about the state of our economy are made daily, but my background, you see, my worldview, renders me unable to take such predictions seriously.

Oh, please don't think I haven't guilt; I have. Plenty. Sometimes. Not always, you're thinking, not enough. But there are moments, rare and brief, when even in the sunshine my body trembles, grows frail from the weight of my burden of guilt, since I'm not ignorant. I read newspapers, watch television. Don't laugh at me. . . . I converse with informed people, and I'm well aware that there's great poverty in this world, in this very country, in fact. Yet, always, I feel sheltered and secure. At least during daylight hours. Aren't I one of the most confident women you've met, isn't that part of what drew you to me last week?

Dominick and I met when I was just a girl, and I wanted him immediately. There were no suffering days, no long nights spent pining: he wanted me, too, and so neither of us experienced a single moment of unrequited love. Just as I'd wanted other things and received them, I received him. Our courtship lacked nothing: it was friendly and pleasant, yet filled with passion and romance. Like best friends, we played tennis and squash in the mornings; like the wildest of young lovers we exchanged erotic Valentine's Day gifts; and, of course, like partners in business, we agreed upon fidelity, loyalty, and the sharing of the fruits of his breadwinning.

And so you wonder why I'm doing this. Why I'm breathless, nervous, on my third drink in too short a time, watching you lean back and cross one leg over the other, then tilt your head in a way I've already noted as a fetching idiosyncracy. Because of what happens at bedtime. Because Dominick hasn't been enough, somehow, although I don't blame him; he couldn't have been. No, I'm not talking about love! Other things . . .

I'll tell you only this about him . . . Dominick, too, is from affluence, from a family a bit more opulent in their display; their money is, after all, more recent, not quite as secure. My parents liked him from the start, approved wholeheartedly of the marriage; their prejudices, although few, are overt, and newer money is not among them. Dominick tells me anecdotes (like my father, he's soft-spoken) about his mother's matching mauve furniture and checkered-wallpapered bathroom, and I have to laugh. Which brings me to the point: it's sometimes during those moments when he and I laugh together, that I tremble, not only with the spasms of laughter.

He and I have plans to travel next month. If you're still part of my life by then . . . and I hope so much that you will be! I know you'll be! . . . we'll have to bear the separation for a few weeks. Won't that be difficult? It's our second vacation this year. We're flying to Europe. I'll miss you constantly, and I'll wonder, over dinner with Dominick, what you're doing at that very minute. I won't feel guilty about you . . . about us. No, I'll just wonder what you do during your own vacations. The first time I was whirled off to Europe, I was twelve, dressing in skirts well above my knees, learning to enjoy a continental breakfast. Now it's a back yard to me, a given, my deserved playground. A right.

Now you're thinking I'm callous. But you've been with me . . . you know I'm not callous, not cold. Perhaps you think I'm ignorant then, despite the *New York Times* and a Wellesley degree? I'm not, I assure you.

Anyway, it's nighttime, as I said, that concerns me most of all, and precisely because I'm not callous or ignorant, I want you to understand. At night, whether I'm in a strange hotel room or in our own bedroom, whether I'm by myself the nights when Dominick's away on business, or whether we're together, side by side, I have to hug myself, grasp myself, tightly, apply pressure to myself, *hurt* myself, even, sometimes, during the very worst nights, in order to sleep. Do you see what I'm talking about? Sleep doesn't come easily to me, despite how easily everything else has come. No, that's an understatement, almost a lie, it's so mild. What I'm trying to tell you is that I fight a raging battle to stay awake each night—yes, it scares Dominick to death, sometimes, which isn't at all fair, because his own sleep is placid. I don't want to sleep and yet I have to . . . and when I finally give in, or when *it* finally gives in, whichever way it works that night, I *hate* it! I might kick, flail, punch, scratch with my fingernails. I might cry out. Do you understand that I might kick at you and wake you out of your deepest sleep, that I might even hurt you? And I might be asleep when I do it, or I might be awake. Certainly Dominick and I have thought about separate beds, but that would make it much, much worse for me, and I'm not sure how much more I could take.

So if I should do something to you tonight, it's not a statement about you. It's not even *me*! At least not the me you met last week. You must understand that I was brought up never to show anger, never to be violent. Never to hate! Occasionally I might admit to a tame dislike, to a moment of condescension, perhaps, but never to hatred, which is reserved for bullies on street corners. But at night, I hate.

What I'm hoping to be able to tell you . . . and it's difficult, because we don't know each other well enough yet, although we will soon, we will know each other more than intimately . . . is that, during sleep, I think that the thing that happens that changes everything is that I *want* something. Or maybe I want two things or twenty things or a hundred things. . . . Things I can't have, don't have. But the worst part, what's tearing at me, is that in the morning, I can't remember what it was that I had wanted enough to fight for. And I can't remember who it is that is keeping me from getting what I want—who it is that I hate so much.

Fortunately, daylight always arrives. Tangible and airy. Fiery sun. Birds. Dominick sipping coffee, then shaving, the familiar buzz of his electric razor, the purr of his car warming up in the garage. And in daytime activities, I'm quite fluent. In my exercise class I stand out, making so many of the other women seem less . . . graceful. You'll be reassured tomorrow morning, I promise you. There I'll be, rubbing sleep from my eyes, sexy, affectionate . . . we'll go out for a light breakfast, and then I'll see you off and we'll make plans for next time. In the daytime I'm really quite fluent, as I've said, and as you've already seen, so there's really nothing for you to worry about. What happens in the darkness doesn't matter. I just wanted to tell you about who I am and what my life has been so that you may draw your own conclusions. . . . In fact, I am far more than fluent . . . I am usually so much in control, so aware and confident, that perhaps *blessed* is a better word.

Or perhaps it is entirely the wrong word, the worst word possible. I'm never quite sure. And now, do, please, tell me what you think.

THE MARRIAGE OF
AN AFTERNOON

I was taking a bath when my wife Sandy walked in wearing only a pair of white bikini underpants decorated with red and blue stars. Our cat had scratched her the day before; the scratch was long and slanted, under her breast. She sat down on the tile floor next to the bathtub. Usually she didn't have the patience just to sit quietly with me. I was happy to have her there.

"Your hair looks very nice in braids," I told her.

"Do I look like Heidi?"

"Who is Heidi?"

"A little blonde Swiss girl. There's a book about her, and if you haven't read it by fifth grade, you're sent to reform school. Her grandfather is this beer-guzzling mountain climber with the hots for her. I guess that in the school you attended, it wasn't required reading."

I dunked my head under the water and closed my eyes. My hair spread out, thick and heavy. It has not thinned, even now.

"Poor Miguel," she said. "He drowned."

I sat up straighter; she took my hand and kissed it as she went on. "Miguel drowned and was unrecognizable afterwards—a bloated, mottled corpse. His young wife, a vivacious blonde, at least a decade younger, came to the funeral wearing faded blue jeans. 'He liked me natural,' she told the reporters. And 'We never had intercultural problems,' she added, 'because I adore fried bananas, and he made an apple pie you wouldn't believe!' And even today, she cries each time she cuts an onion." She stroked my forehead, getting herself wet. "Do you love me?"

"Always. *Te quiero. Te adoro.*" I touched the scratch. "Does it hurt you?"

"No. Yesterday it hurt, but today I feel nothing." She put her hand into the water, and then touched her fingers to her mouth. "Miguel, I think I'll write a story and send it to the *Reader's Digest*, title it, 'I Am Sandy's Motivation For Marrying (at such a young age) This Miguel.'"

"*Por que?*" I loved talking Spanish to her, loved when she answered me in it.

"It'll be a shocking story, sordid, ribald . . . unlike the usual *Reader's Digest* stuff. Because . . . I want the world to know of the phallic shotgun pointed in my ribs, and the man who kept saying, 'Marry me and I geev you ze stars, ze moon, all ze marijuana fields in South America.'"

"That's a French accent."

She laughed. "Mostly I did it because it was a lark. He seemed exotic, and because it irritated the hell out of my parents! I meant no harm, of course."

My wet hair covered my eyes. "Do you want to wash my hair for me?"

"No."

"Why not? You love it when I do it for you."

"Well, I guess that I *like* the sensation I get when someone else massages my scalp and towels me dry and kisses my neck, my shoulders. . . . But where is the equivalent sensation if I do it for you?"

I saw now that she had come into the bathroom to play games with me, like the child she was. I felt a tenderness.

"You judge me too often, Señor. My lawyer is out of town, playing backgammon in Los Angeles, arranging some quickies in Reno."

She put her face in the water and kissed my belly.

"Why don't you kiss me all over?" No woman before or since has kissed me like my wife, the small Sandrita. Those kisses came from somewhere. I leaned back for her, watching her lift her head out of the water, watching her eyes open.

"Why don't you shave your hair off," she said.

She stood up and walked to the medicine chest, the water dripping from her hair onto her back and onto the red and blue stars as she peered into the chest. She walked toward me, holding my razor. The water had begun turning cold. She kneeled by the tub again and said, "Miguel, please shave." Then, "*Por favor, mi esposo, mi popi, toda tus pelos*. All of it. *Para mi*."

I took the razor. This young girl was legally my wife (we'd met at a party—me with my camera around my neck, so uncertain of my English, so taken by her words, her tiny halter top) and yet I was just part of a dream she had one night. In Bolivia my mother and sisters shared their dreams at breakfast, and the cards and the stars in the evenings. But Sandy grew up, grew bored of her dream. My mother and sisters never grow tired of dreaming. Sandy was not like them. "I may dream my life away," she said one time, "but the dreams must change." But back then her dream was still so strong that I held that razor in my hand.

She handed me the soap and I began to lather the hairs on my belly. "I'm doing this for you, Sandrita," I said. "I'm going to be bald all over, like a woman. This is proof of my love, my honesty. How could I show myself to anyone else but you if I look like this? This is all for you."

She didn't say anything, not then, not even as I worked my way down. The hairs were floating in the water around me. My wife, Sandra, lifted out a few and placed them along the edge of the tub where they curled up like little pigs' tails and remained for days.

A COMB AND A SNAKE

During an argument, Eve threw his metal comb into the toilet bowl and flushed. Adam turned red. "You loon," he muttered. "Now the toilet will be stopped up, and for what? What did you prove?"

A week later, Eve decided to start spending more time alone, doing things, rediscovering herself. Adam agreed that time alone might be beneficial for her—perhaps the one lacking ingredient. "Someone whose diet lacks one vitamin," he elaborated, "initially requires massive doses to compensate." An article she'd recently come across in her favorite magazine reinforced the decision. While they spoke, she went from room to room watering—but carefully not overwatering—her many plants which so filled the apartment that drapes and chairs were chosen to match.

She spent the next Saturday wandering through the city, following the plan which had been outlined in the magazine—the Whitney, a dimly lit West Village cafe, a new Mexican crafts boutique. By late afternoon, she was walking closer to the buildings, starting at loud noises. When darkness fell, she entered a theater on Third Avenue to see a new film which had been reviewed in the same issue of the magazine. The movie ended on a sad note, with the young, dewey-eyed heroine tearfully choosing to have an abortion. Immediately Eve was out the door of the theater, hailing a taxi, conscious of weakness in her legs, of the sudden rain splattering and frizzing her long hair, of the dangers of dark city streets.

Adam was watching Audie Murphy on channel five, eating applesauce in the dark. "All right," he said, placing his bowl and spoon upon the table.

She trembled (although she'd been gone less than a full day) for the African violet, caressing first a leaf, then the stem.

They went to bed.

Still, the comb had been flushed, and the toilet now continually overflowed. Going to the bathroom in the mornings and evenings had become so harrowing that between the hours of nine and five, while at their respective jobs, they relished the use of office facilities.

Eve resisted calling the landlord, although Adam wanted to. The landlord lived on the ground floor, and at the age of eighty-six still performed all repairs himself. "I'm not trusting blacks," he would say when an impatient tenant demanded either more professional or more expedient service. "Move across the street if you want blacks playing with your things."

One morning the landlord approached Eve. "So you got a comb stuck."

She was climbing the stairs, carrying a newly purchased hair rinse she'd seen advertised on television; Adam was jogging in the park. "One of our little nephews threw it down, we couldn't stop him in time."

The next morning the landlord arrived, uncalled for, bearing what he called his "snake-tool."

"My nephew . . ." Eve began.

"Nah! Your husband already told me it was you in some kind of fit."

At noon Adam returned from the barber shop. He had forgotten to stop at The Greenery for a new flowerpot.

"The landlord was here, but he couldn't get the comb out," she told him, noting immediately the one flyaway hair in his trimmed mustache. "He said it won't require a plumber, though. He pushed it down, or something."

"He's lying. It's a *metal* comb—it might mean the total removal of the tank! We sure as hell can't afford to pay for that!"

They borrowed the landlord's snake one day when he was out. Clumped dark hairs attached themselves to the snake, but no comb.

"They're yours," Adam said.

She wanted to swoon. White tiles, white walls, dark hairs . . . why didn't someone just call a plumber?

He shoved the snake in deeper, turning it around and around and around, hoping to somehow connect with the metal comb. "This is absurd," he blurted, instantly sorry.

The snake became a permanent fixture; the landlord never asked for it back. Once a week, at least, her husband had to swish it about, just to insure that the flush mechanism worked at all.

"The landlord told me that you were embarrassed to admit it was you who threw the comb down there," Adam mentioned one night as they lay in bed, both sweating and irritated because of the heat and the noise of fire engines. "You should have admitted it."

Eve said nothing, thinking about the survival of her more fragile plants during such a heat spell, dreading ugly brown patches.

"I know he's furious," Adam went on, "because he's beginning to see that we'll need outside help."

The next morning, the toilet belched and bubbled.

"You do it for once," Adam decided, thrusting the snake into her hands.

Almost immediately Eve heard the click and knew that somehow the horizontal metal comb had at long last attached itself to the coiled metal snake. Impossible—physically impossible!—but true. She twisted the handle in circles until the comb began surfacing. Adam was silent. The only sound was metal against porcelain.

The comb was sparkling, and during its immersion had radically altered in appearance: no longer straight and pointed, each tooth of the comb had been transformed into a distinct letter of the alphabet, together boldly completing two separate words and one mark of punctuation—

LEAVE NOW!

—causing her, right there on the spot, to nod just once, ferociously, at Adam.

He stood still, with his arms at his sides in his own bathroom: beginning to make silent plans to divide the furniture and appliances, to readjust to the bachelor's life: advertisements for liberated singles, "personals" from widows and divorcees, frozen French toast breakfasts.

Eve knew, and Adam knew, that although there had not been anything specifically wrong, that although there was no one evening to which she absolutely would be able to point a finger years later in an analyst's office, still, once a comb and a snake have spoken so precisely and clearly to even a vaguely unhappy wife, a woman with no particular plans in the offing, it is no longer a matter of an imbalanced diet, of too much protein, not enough carbohydrates, starches or Vitamin E.

She felt herself destined and eager to be off, ready to pack up her dresses, shoes, pocketbooks, the natural bristle hairbrush, even the tortoise-shell hairclips (an anniversary gift). The plants would go to friends and relatives. She would learn to be content without the green leaves and purple buds each morning, without the bright ceramic watering can beside her bed. Perhaps she'd buy some tight jersey turtlenecks, cut her hair in a freer style.

Almost in unison they took deep breaths, after which, both suddenly feeling elated and ravenous, they ran side by side into the kitchen. Flinging open the refrigerator door, they each grabbed a juicy red apple. They took large bites, gulped air, and then took larger and larger bites.

THE RESOLUTION
OF MUSCLE

S ylvia Plath writes, in *The Bell Jar*, that the years of her
life stretched out before her like telephone poles, end to end.

I see it more this way: the years ahead are before me,
each one in the shape of dumbbells or a Universal machine
in a gym.

I see it this way: bench press, shoulder press, leg
press . . .

Like Sylvia Plath was, I'm young enough, still, even
though I'm not that young any more, let's face it, to make
momentous changes, earth-shattering decisions. So . . . I can
do high repetitions with low weights and grow thinner and
trim down and tone up . . . or I can do high weights and low
reps and grow muscular. Achieve definition. *Real muscles*.

I can PUMP UP!

Some day I might even enter a show, a competition, and pump up those muscles, wearing a revealing bikini, showing lots of sinewy flesh. Nothing like sashaying along a beach having men ogling me. . . . This would be like . . . like *work*! I'd be AT WORK! Displaying the body that I'd worked so hard to achieve! It would be like being told by the boss that you're indispensable, or by your students that you're the best teacher they've ever had. Not like a sex show, in other words. A MUSCLE SHOW!

But I've got three children, a husband, parents in Forest Hills. What will they all think?

Honey, my husband says, sure, tone up, firm up, trim down . . . not that you don't look fine the way you are, of course . . .

Of course.

Mommy, say my three children in unison, how come you're never around making brownies for us any more? WHERE ARE OUR BROWNIES?

What in the world, says my mother, do you want to do that sort of thing for? Can't you . . . find something else to do with your free time?

Free time?

My father, he's silent. He always was.

My best friend, she says, you've got to resolve this one way or the other. What's this business of sneaking off to candy stores to look at muscle men in magazines?

Hey, it's not the men, I insist . . .

Sylvia Plath, I understand, was not especially muscular. This is not meant as a strike against her. Obviously, she had something else to do with her free time. Not bench press, shoulder press, leg press . . .

I copied from her. From Sylvia. I wrote a poem. It needs work, of course, but it is a poem. My poem.

FOR SYLVIA

On a moonlit night when all was
                calm
Something happened down on the
                farm
A young girl lifted one too many
                bales of hay
Her body filled out, her muscles
                said Hey!
On a moonlit night in the middle
                of the city
Something happened to a girl very
                pretty.
She went to the grocery and bought
                Daddy's six-pack,
And when she got home, this girl was
                stacked
                with
                muscles
                shouting
                Hey!

There's a group of us at the gym: Laura, Sandy, Dotty, Belinda, and me. . . . We're the early evening gang. The men have a separate room.

Laura: I'm mostly working on
my inner thighs and fanny. . . .
I was thin in high school. . . .
My husband, well, we're separated . . . he's
muscular, and I emulate him.

Sandy: I'm a big girl, but flat chested.
So I do lots of stuff for the
pecs. . . . Bench presses and a
trillion pully things. . . . It's all
embarrassing!

Dotty: I'm thirty-six and already
my doctor says watch out, not much
longer. The other women are extremely
supportive. I don't look in the
mirror.

Belinda: First I tried running, I
hurt my knee. Then I swam, but
I'm allergic to chlorine. Some of
the women's magazines said why not
try this, so I figured okay, why not?
I hate it, every minute of it.

So, you see, none of them exactly share my problem.
None of them are pressed to resolve an issue right away like I
am. High reps and low weights or low reps and high weights?
It's a dilemma. I can change the course of my life, create myself
anew, either way. EITHER WAY! My God! But which way? How
shall I be born again?

MUSCLES are so seductive. They seduce me. They infil-
trate my dreams.

Also, I wrote a song. It needs work, too, but, still, it's
my song.

RESOLUTION

*(to be sung by a chorus of
five women: one short and
muscular, wearing a
bikini; one tall and thin,
wearing running shorts and
sneakers; one fleshy and
voluptuous, wearing a low-cut
satin gown; one angular, wearing
a flowered shirtwaist dress;*

one elegant, wearing all black,
with her face veiled)

Each of us has a problem
Somewhere in our souls. . . .
Each of us has had to face something
Has had to change, to mold, to bend, to
　　grow.
Oooo . . . Oooo . . . Oooo . . .

Who may we turn to for advice
When life seems hard and without
　　peace. . . .
Each of us has had to seek help from
　　somewhere
Has had to ask and plead and query and
　　persist.
Oooo . . . Oooo . . . Oooo . . .

When we were young we climbed tele-
　　phone poles
And trees and played with rocking horses
　　and dolls. . . .
Now we are older and our joints are stiff
And dolls remind us too much of our
　　children.
Oooo . . . Oooo . . . Oooo.

Sometimes I feel very alone. So very alone. We live in
a house not far from the bus line, though. It was my grand-
parents' house until their deaths. I feel them in every room,
every corner, every dust particle. Spooky. But it doesn't make
me feel less alone. My children leave their things all over the
house. That also doesn't make me feel less alone.

My husband wrote me a note one day. He left it by the
phone:

Dear, whatever you decide to do, we will be behind
you, you know that. Keep up the good work. Your
family is your friend!

But that still doesn't help with the issue. The issue remains. I am going to do it—to do SOMETHING—one way or another. No matter what. They misunderstand the issue. They might think my issue is slight. They're wrong. It's deceptive, and big. Which way? Low weights, high reps; high weights, low reps?

Fashion magazines or muscle magazines?

No magazines at all?

Shall I just wing it, play it by ear, see what happens, do it by mood, by color, by weather, by poem, by song?

So. What is the resolution? I've read all of Sylvia Plath's poetry and decided she was quite credible. And interesting. And enticing. I empathize more than you might think. But I do wish that she had just once done some leg and bench presses, some bicep curls and tricep extensions. Who knows what might have happened then? That's how large this issue could be, you see.

I resolve . . . I resolve . . .

To be strong . . . for starters. To press . . . forward.

THE COUNTRY IN MAURA

First, the introductions: I'm a woman, an observer, an acquaintance of Maura's. My hair is curly; my feet are size six and a half; I don't always wear a bra, but usually I do. You're a male. My guess is that you wear eyeglasses which add to your scholarly attractiveness; you jog regularly, but don't bore people at parties with the details; you're young, still in your thirties, finishing a dissertation at a well-known, liberal university, in a field related to my own. We are both innovators, contemporary Fultons mocked for our intellectual follies. We are serious scholars who believe in astrology, who consult the I Ching, who interpret paper fortunes in Chinese restaurants far more seriously than our suburban parents ever expected us to.

Recently, someone you respect a great deal mentioned to you that I was observing a living female subject in order to extract metaphors about contemporary culture. My name was unfamiliar to you, and although our universities are located in cities far from one another, you were intrigued. Despite the rough schedule you must keep, despite the fact that you must often juggle complete exhaustion with a manic cerebral energy. You were intrigued enough to type a letter asking me to send as much work as I have ready, assuring me that there's no competition, no possible plagiarism involved, that we are peers, not enemies.

Your letter made me feel warm, cuddly, snug. I am not, then, working in a vacuum. I imagine that you have a classic nose and chin, that you wear beige Levis and plaid flannel shirts with metal snaps.

Following are some of the notes I've taken about Maura, and some of the hypotheses I've drawn. Please note that nothing has been formalized, that, in fact, I may never choose to formalize these in the standard academic form. Haven't you been feeling the same way? After all, our ideas are outside the mainstream.

Also, I collect menus from diners along highways. Those plastic menus which express great truths: "Mike's Famous Chili, Hotter'n Mom Ever Made It." "The Kitchen Sink Sundae smug . . . Are You Man Enough To Eat It?"

But the menus must wait, until this first paper is completed and published; for the time being, my research deals exclusively with Maura and her music; the menus are tomorrow. Please read the enclosed and feel free, if you would, to comment. This is a Xeroxed copy.

Introduction

Turn on the radio. Between the commercials, the incorrect traffic and weather reports, the witty disk jockey vs. newscaster banter, the witty disk jockey vs. jocular weather-girl banter, you can still hear the songs. Music. Feet still dance, fingers still tap.

Turn on the radio. You're making love to someone. Or
just having sex, perhaps. Have I just offended you by using
the word "just?" I take it back. Why should sex, as opposed
to love, be "just?" But you do know that moment, the moment during which you're passionately involved, caught in
that rare and beautiful embrace, the stuff of poetry, the
matter of art through the ages, when a song—Mick Jagger,
Tony Bennett, Duke Ellington, the Talking Heads—the mere
background noise, becomes the focus of your attention. "I love
you," says the person atop you, or "You're the best," whispers
the person beneath you, but the only voice you hear is that of
a crooning male informing you that he left his heart in San
Francisco.

Now shut off the radio. Concentrate. Consider how much
more the death of Elvis Presley moved you than the death of
Chairman Mao. Think of how those aging radicals wept for
Paul Robeson. The jazz world mourned over Bessie and Billie;
the whole world mourned over John Lennon.

Keep the radio down low. You've finally found the one
person to whom you feel forever bound. (You know, though,
that too soon will come the battles over who does the dishes,
who is less giving in the bedroom, who made the $19.12 phone
call to Detroit, and that you'll develop wrinkles, ulcers, possible
migraines, probable infidelities.) Still, for now, you are bound
to this unique individual. Confess, confess that you and he/she
"have a song." A special song. *Your* song. "Hush! They're
playing our song . . ." you've cooed, haven't you?

Over the low buzz of soft music, I hear a voice of protest. "Excuse me," someone smugly intones, "but I'm tone
deaf!" Harumph, that person thinks, music ain't got no part
in my life! Bah! That flimsy excuse merely adds fuel to my
fire! Tone deaf? The tone deaf often sing the most beautifully.
In Times Square, on Sunset Strip, in downtown Sioux City, the
berserk, the bombed-out, carrying their shopping bags filled
with soiled garter belts, moldy chicken wings, and vinyl dolls,
always sing.

"Ave Maria," "Blowing in the Wind," "Gloomy Sunday,"
"The Cowman and the Farmer Should be Friends," "Salt Pea-

nuts," "Barnacle Bill, the Sailor," "I Love Paris in the Springtime;" the list is endless.

To summarize: the music, these ditties, these tunes, these be-bop-diddy-ops of our lives are, in fact, our very lives. (Just as "The Kitchen Sink Sundae" and "The Hottest Chili in Town" are, but they must wait for now.) A second hypothesis: if the songs are our lives, and the singers are the songs (and you've acknowledged the truth of that age-old adage long before this) we are also the singer. We never think of hound dogs, we think of Elvis, his stance, his body, his sneer. We think of Judy's struggle with pills, not rainbows. Frank and the Mafia, not strangers in the night. Dean and his drinking problem, not pizzas in the sky. The singer, the song, the listener. Bear this triangle in mind as you read Maura's story.

The Story of Maura

She would wail D-I-V-O-R-C-E at all hours along with Tammy on tape. She would languish in a tub, soaping her legs, lathering her belly, while Loretta sang "Coal Miner's Daughter." Her hair, previously a subtle sort of career-woman pageboy, became overnight an elaborate coiffure of curls, ribbons, and bows; her tapered, lined pantsuit suddenly boasted spangles and studs. The grey herringbone winter vest was splashy with a rhinestone border and dangling beads.

People worried. But Maura sat, enamored of Dolly, dreaming nightdreams and daydreams in which Merle, a lithe, wiry trucker, would pick her up at the truckstop diner. She was the waitress, of course, wearing a tighter-than-tight white polyester dress, shorter-than-short, showing off her great legs. She slapped fried eggs onto plates, dumped scoops of vanilla ice cream beside man-portions of deep-dish apple pie with a crust too thick for the weak in arm. (The menu read, "Our Apple Pie A La Mode—Mom Baked It, Men Eat It.") So there she'd be, slapping down some dish or other (hash browns, pork chops with applesauce, salad with Eye-talian dressing) when she'd sense "his" eyes upon her. Merle. Staring in his special, dark-eyed, on-the-road man's way. And he'd be there later, waiting,

unannounced but certainly not unexpected, when she got off at
seven, and he'd climb into his truck, and they'd hit a bar or two
and dance—he was a smooth dancer—and maybe he'd let her,
just for a second on the way to the motel, just for a second as a
joke, talk into his CB radio. "This is . . ." she giggled.

"Think of a handle." Merle stroked her stockinged thigh.
"You gotta have a handle."

"This is," Maura whispered in her dream, "Hot-to-Trot."

And they'd shut off the CB real quick, before someone
could answer.

She and Merle made love later that night, a special kind
of love, better than regular, because he'd be back on the road by
morning, and because, somewhere in some part of the country,
there was a wife and a house not yet paid for and a boy in the
sixth grade named Merle, Jr.

Maura was twenty-nine years old when this fever hit her.
She was single, living in a small apartment in a building with
a doorman named Angel. Her college degree was in English
literature. She was sharp, pretty, working as an executive
secretary for an editor in a major publishing house. Maura
loved to dance in discos with handsome men in tight pants
and shining shoes. Her phone manners were perfect, her
mind organized, her typing accurate at 85 wpm. She read
magazines, remembered facts, and could chat with the authors
who occasionally had to wait for the editor.

Maura had a number of girlfriends in whom she confided
the details of her days. Nan was her closest friend. They shared
lunch hours, chatting over Bloody Marys, guacamole, carrot
cake, and black coffee. (Yes, I envy Maura and her friends.
My present lifestyle in the graduate department keeps me
alone most of the time. A close girlfriend to share a cafeteria
hamburger with? To chat about menu lore, singers and songs?
Only in my dreams . . .)

Maura dated often and had been in love once, with a
salesman from New Rochelle. It hadn't worked out.

And then, suddenly, the fever struck. The editor was
concerned.

"If I'd wanted to hire a Dolly Parton look-alike," he

confided to the executive editor, "I would have advertised for one. What do you think is going on?"

"It must be love," suggested the executive editor, who was female. "What else?"

Nan was blunt over a Friday afternoon lunch of avocado salad and white wine. "What gives?"

"I don't know. What?" asked Maura, thinking she'd just been asked a riddle. Nan shook her head, dolefully dipping an avocado slice into the garlic and herb dressing.

A few days later the office telephone rang. Maura was supposed to answer the editor's telephone when it rang. But this particular day—in the midst of Dolly / Loretta / Tammy fever—she was polishing her fingernails. The color was Vivid Violet. The telephone rang and rang and then was silent.

The next day the editor brought an important author into the office. "Maura," her boss began, "this is John," Roland, the author of . . ."

"Oh, I'd a'known you *anywhere*, Mr. Roland," beamed Maura. "I seen your picture in that Sunday magazine. Howdee," and she became suddenly demure, mascaraed eyes downcast.

The editor took John Roland into his office and closed the door.

Of course, you're wondering by now, exactly what my relationship is to Maura. I knew her. In a sense, I'll always know her. Perhaps she's the best friend my lifestyle doesn't allow. Actually, I'd met her years before through someone else, and then, that someone else (my mother) informed me of Maura's fever when it struck. And so I contacted her and observed. I observed rationally, discreetly, not unkindly. But it wasn't until I questioned her at length one evening, after a few glasses of vermouth, that I learned of her visions. Her visions are recorded forever on the tape recorder I'd carried along: her dreamy voice, her intense rambling.

Yes, Maura had visions: She, in a gingham dress, almost a pinafore, with puffy sleeves and lace around the hem, po' girl sandals on her feet, but heck, who cares, she had sunshine, blue skies, and most of all, her man; and he may just be an elevator operator in a big, fancy office building downtown, but

he was her man and he didn't cheat. On Friday nights, after his
hard working week, they went to the local tavern and danced
and whooped and hollered up a storm, and the baby-sitter, a
real smart gal, maybe she'd even go to college someday, baby-
sat for the kids and read to them from the Good Book.

A bit more erotic a vision: She, on the hog farm, sittin'
there in her cut-off blue-jean short shorts, with the fringes
cascading from a jagged hem, amidst the pigs, oh-so-down-
home, y'all come back here, legs crossed so you could see
a wee bit, just a wee bit, not too much, and she with the
tangled wild hair of the poor farm gal, she with the full lips
of innocence and rural fantasies.

Wholesome vision: Riding in the newly purchased (on
credit), used pick-up. But their credit in town was sound; why,
she or Bill could just walk into the bank and have a loan in
seconds flat, their credit was so good! They'd had it painted
red, although she thought it maybe a bit too flamboyant, but
Bill laughed and said, "Honey, if we have it, let's flaunt it!" and
she'd laughed, happy to see him so boyish and impulsive, just
like in the old days. Now it was Sunday morning, and she was
waving to the neighbors, exchanging Howdees and See You At
Churches and See You Tonight At The Pot Lucks. Little Bill,
Jr. and 'Retta sitting all fancied up in their Sunday best ('Retta
looking like an angel, worth taking out the Instamatic for) all
going to hear the new preacher.

Then, a few weeks after Maura's confession, just when
the editor was considering letting her go, the visions stopped.
Maura became Maura again. Just like that. On a Wednesday
morning she arrived at work with a carefully combed pageboy,
a wine-colored scarf tossed around her neck, and polished
high-heeled leather boots. Subtle lipstick shaded her lips,
which were no longer the large, wet things they'd become;
instead, they were the pursed, thinner lips of a crackerjack,
well-groomed, self-starting executive secretary of a major publishing house.

The editor gave her a bonus. Still, he was very curious.
"What was all that?" he asked.

"What was all what?"

He decided certain things were better left unknown. Without proofreading, he added his signature to the typed letters she handed him.

An Interpretation of Maura's Story

Is there, we must ask, a moral to this tale? Immediately, the jaded critics out there will scoff at the idea that I wish to investigate the morality of this story. To those people I offer the following hypothesis, one which I hope to defend at length in the final version of this paper: there is a moral in every story, a moral in every object, in every song, in every word, and in every glance.

So. Let us first examine the "meaning" to us of Maura, the woman. In order to accomplish this, I suggest that it is first necessary to examine the women that she chose to emulate. (The Singers, not merely the Song.)

Dolly: From a poor home, she has suffered. A very, very poor home, had to wear a coat patched together from pieces of old quilts and curtains, but she thought the coat was beautiful because her mother had made it with her own working woman's hands. Now Dolly wears wigs, wigs galore, buttons, bows, frills, laces, tight sexpot clothes, to make up for those deprived years when she slept on urine-stained sheets and couldn't afford a pink ribbon for her pigtails. The fans love her wigs. They fetishize her buttons, her bows, her bountiful breasts.

Loretta: From a poor home, she has suffered. A very, very poor home, she didn't always have shoes. Her daddy was nearly a saint down there in the coal mines. She also couldn't afford a pink ribbon for her pigtails. But now she has long chestnut hair and a personal hairdresser, a huge bus filled with musicians who cater to her nervous ways, lots of kids, and she owns the town of Hurricane Hills, Tennessee. The fans love her tight-at-the-waist high-collared dresses, her adoring grandchildren, and her tendency to fall to pieces.

Tammy: She too has suffered. She tells us of the problem of lovin' a drinkin', cheatin' husband, and of the difficulties of reconciling Christianity with womanhood. The fans love her long, teased hair, her ideas about putting Jesus on television, the pain in her eyes, and the thick eye makeup that doesn't mask the pain.

A pattern, obviously. Not clones, but mythic characters, perhaps. You asked in your letter that I send you what was completed of my work, and this is it. I've not endeavored yet, to draw a final conclusion about Maura's story, because my research is not done. Daily I seek for clues in the Greek literature, in the Roman comedies, the Elizabethan tragedies. Daily I come closer.

I'll venture one more hypothesis, though: Maura is not a unique case in contemporary times! There are others, women around the world, experiencing this to lesser and greater degrees. (Naturally, I intend to develop this idea in the final version of this paper.)

Recently I called Maura, curious to see if there had been any relapses or new insights. I was connected to a recording of her voice. "Hi, this is Maura. I'm sorry, but I'm out having a fabulous time. So just leave your name and number at the sound of the beep. . . ."

The next night she called. "I was having dinner with Patti, the new editorial assistant in my division. How are you?"

"Fine."

"Still in grad school?"

"Where else?" I asked. "Maura, I called to find out how you've been feeling all this time since your . . . return?"

"That's all so long ago. Mostly, I remember nothing. I'm happier now, since I jog and was given a raise. Sorry."

And so I hung up after a few more minutes of chit-chat, wishing her the best of luck in all worlds, thanking her for having called me so promptly. Now I continue my research, continue to attempt to survive on the piddling fellowship money. I haven't gained any weight, though I rarely exercise, spending most of my time in my library carrel, or at the desk in my tiny apartment in the graduate student complex. Sending my work to you has been a welcome break. I would love to see some of your own work-in-progress; my phone number is listed. Do you ever get to this part of the country?

I admit to having desires myself. My stereo broke in transit when I moved here, and I can't afford a new one. Radios make me nervous. Occasionally I attend a concert using my student I.D., but, in general, I don't wish to allow music into my life. Why rock the boat? I collect menus, but resist the need to read and reread them nightly. Eventually, when the dissertation is completed, I'll look for a teaching position somewhere.

And I wish you the best of luck in your particular field, as I sit here combing my curling auburn tresses, putting a bit of rouge on my cheeks, knowing that we make our choices, that we listen to music and eat at diners according to our preferences, that we choose classical or bebop, bagels or muffins, butter or jam, loneliness or love. And *you* are free, as I've said, to choose to keep in touch.

TO BOSTON

U sually she sat, nearly motionless, for the first five, or
even ten minutes, staring at the fading beige rug, or at
the Wyeth print on the wall, but today it was obvious that
she wanted to begin at once: the way she first drummed her
fingers along the chair edge, then twisted the three silver
Mexican rings she wore, next touched one, then the other,
of her filigreed earrings, intertwining them with her long and
wavy hair.

So he sat, waiting as always, letting the mood of the client
set the tone, at least initially, of the session. And she was a particularly moody girl, had been from the first day when she'd
entered and asked in a way he'd since come to think as of her
own distinctly coy, yet somehow, hostile, manner, "Before we
begin, I'd like to know what your degree is in, and which of
the grand old shrinks is your guru."

His reply that he had an M.A. in social work and was working toward a Ph.D. in psychology and (perhaps a bit too quickly and defensively) that she needn't worry, despite his age he'd worked with a good many clients already, had left her with a quizzical, dissatisfied expression, as though she'd been expecting more, or something else. He'd asked her why she'd come.

"Well," she'd answered, looking away, seeming like a nineteen-year-old at last, exhibiting the nervousness which was natural during her first visit, "I don't know. My mother insisted I come because of certain things which have displeased her, and which she won't tell my father about, on the condition that I have the 'help of a professional.'" Mimicking the tone of her mother, her confidence and sarcasm had returned. Even now, five months later, she had yet to reveal what the "certain things" were.

It had been a slow five months, he thought, but not without many good moments. And so he waited, feeling her need to begin, although still she sat silently, staring into "Christina's World." Often, the breathy way she spoke, placing stress on unusual syllables, with sudden theatrical gestures, reminded him of one of those popular contemporary actresses, deliberately innocent, naively seductive. But he stopped himself from that kind of projection: she was, after all, only a junior in college, from a middle-income background, a girl with a lot of problems to be worked through, and a long way from working through them.

"What's that bracelet you've got on?" she began, slowly taking her leave of Christina.

"This?" He was surprised. He'd always worn the bracelet. "It means I'm allergic to penicillin." He waited once again, but she said nothing, nor did her expression. "If I'm ever in an accident, or fall ill in a public place, any doctor would know not to administer penicillin to me." His eagerness to follow her mood was difficult to control.

"Because I've been wondering," she said, "if that was some kind of religious symbol engraved in it, and if secretly you belonged to some kind of bizarre sect . . . like the ones in black

robes and silver crosses who say they're collecting for retard-
ed children." She bent down to untie and retie the shoelaces
of her brown moccasins before continuing. "But now I know
what you mean. I read a *Reader's Digest* this-happened-to-me
article in the gynecologist's office last year by some woman
who opened her door to find her husband on the front steps
with a swollen grey neck and bulging eyes, in the throes of
penicillin shock. . . . Listen, I was just being feisty about the
bracelet, trying to start an argument, because really I have
something important to say: I won't be coming back for
any more sessions. This is my last one. Because I'm getting
married."

"Okay," he thought. "Okay." He leaned back, took a deep
breath as he'd trained himself to do. "To *who?*"

"To *whom*," she corrected. according to their one standing joke which had its origins about two months before when
she, the English major, had corrected a change of tense in his
speech, haughtily stating, "If you aren't aware of proper sen-
tence construction, how can you be aware of proper people
construction?" His laugh had been so spontaneous and loud
that she'd softened, until grammar eventually became the only
comic relief between them.

He waited, not smiling.

"To someone at school . . . I've been seeing him for about
three months, but I've never told you about him . . ."

"But why not?" This was unimaginable, rendering the five
months of twice weekly sessions a sham. He crossed one leg,
deliberately, over the other, forcing his features to rest, feeling
foolish as his forehead resisted the uncreasing.

"I'm not sure." She stood up. "Listen, I've enjoyed these
sessions in a way. I can't say you've been particularly help-
ful . . . maybe only because I haven't been ready . . . everyone
says you've got to be open to this sort of thing, and since I
was basically forced into it . . ." Quite formally, she held out
her hand.

Refusing to offer his own in response, he shook his head
from side to side. "But . . . you're not ready yet!" There was an
unprofessional note in his voice, along with something almost

like a pout, but he decided what the hell, he'd only been finished with his Master's and working at the Family Center for a little less than a year, during which—he now realized—he'd enjoyed sessions with her a great deal. The other three college-aged girls assigned to him by his supervisor were less than articulate, coming to him because their best girlfriends were in therapy, or because they thought he could answer their questions about birth control, whereas she'd truly seemed to be reaching out, yet always keeping him at bay in a manner he'd been stimulated by. And, of course, he was genuinely concerned about her emotional well-being, about the healing of emotional wounds which had begun early: first, during a childhood in which she'd been punished, spanked, and made to feel clumsy and helpless far too often; soon after, when at fourteen she'd narrowly escaped a rape in a basement of her own building; then at seventeen, when her first boyfriend, an art student, walked out after their third date together, saying, "I'm sorry, it's not that I don't like you, but these experiences leave me cold;" and again, eight months later, when her second boyfriend, after convincing her to try LSD with him during a Sunday afternoon concert in Central Park, had left her on a bench while he wandered off to find an old friend, never to return. These facts about her past had been offered haltingly—each only once—each time in that mocking, breathy voice, with the slight ambiguous curve of the lips; each time she'd reminded him more than ever of that kind of vulnerable yet bitchy actress, the kind who pushes the male lead to both absolute fury and helpless passion. And none of it had been worked through: not her ambivalent feelings toward her despotic father, not her rage and fear about the near-rape, not her reasons for having selected two such irresponsible boyfriends, certainly not her reasons for virtually having withdrawn from any—even platonic—contact with boys her own age since the Central Park incident. Except, he corrected himself, the latter fact wasn't a fact, after all.

Nor had he and she talked enough about the positive things in her life: the fact that her father, despite a temper, seemed hard-working and generous, that her mother (admit-

tedly, not a strong role model) was kind, and that her older
brother was putting himself through law school and earning
straight A's. But what was most positive, it had appeared to
him from the start, was her college career: she was one of
the top English majors in the largest branch of City University,
receiving grades and writing papers that had caused at least
one professor to evince special interest in her, to encourage
graduate school and scholarship applications.

She'd withdrawn her hand and was heading for the door.
Again, he spoke in an unprofessional voice. "But you haven't really *begun* to deal with your feelings about men, and if you're
going to get . . ." He couldn't say the word.

She hesitated. "I know. It seems very strange to you.
You've got a certain perspective, a way of viewing the world,
and you've worked long and hard to be entitled to that perspective. Still, I am discontinuing therapy and I am getting
married. It seems to me that this is the right approach at this
particular point in my life."

For a second he wondered if she were deliberately paro-
dying both himself and his profession, but that wasn't important; what he needed to do was to think fast, to find the right
words to convince her to agree to even just one more session.
But before he had, she smiled awkwardly and let herself out
the door.

The college was sprawling, overcrowded, and beset by
all of the problems, exaggerated, that schools faced all across
the country: changing admissions standards, lack of funds,
disgruntled faculty, alienated students; such a campus would
have permitted her to withdraw by merely filling out a few
sheets of paper with her name, address, student status and
I.D. number, accompanied by the words, "personal reasons,"
yet she felt an obligation to speak to the professor with whom
she'd taken three literature classes, as well as an independent
study, especially since he'd referred to himself a number of
times, as her "mentor."

Conveniently, he was alone in the office he shared with
two other teachers, feet up on his desk, grading basic compo-

sition papers beneath the various Doonesbury cartoons. She
sat across from him, crossing one leg over her thigh, in the
manner she'd consciously begun copying from men on the
subway when she was in junior high school.

"I think you're making a mistake . . . a big mistake," he
said as soon as she'd finished her announcement, immediately
annoyed at himself for the triteness. Still, no other words came.
Lately, he'd been feeling stranded, cut off from his own words
and ideas, bewildered by the disrespect and lack of interest of
so many of his students, and wondering if the two things were
somehow connected. "A mistake you'll regret."

"Nothing is irreparable, is it?" she asked, in that nearly
flirtatious way, couching her words, as always, in a student's diffidence and awkwardness: not looking directly at
him, tossing her hair back and forth, then distractedly biting
her fingernails, so that he could never justifiably think of her
as an out-and-out, bona fide tease, of seeking better grades by
appealing to his vanity.

"I'd say a lot of things are *most* irreparable. My marriage,
for instance, produced Jason. And he's irreparable, isn't he?"

"You love him, don't you? And your ex-wife loves him,
right? What needs repair?"

There she went, doing exactly what irritated him most
about even his good students, *especially* his few good students:
going off on some unrelated tangent, bringing up his son and
ex-wife when what they'd been discussing was *her* decision.
"If you handed in a paper trying to argue a point with that kind
of logic, I'd scrawl in the big, red, professorial letters you know
all too well, 'Illogical, tangential, stick to the point, please!' "

"Okay." She never bothered trying to point out his own
irrationality; too many times she'd observe him lose his train
of thought mid-sentence in class, then continue with an unrelated idea, visibly frightened. More than once he'd scrawled
notes on her papers and exams asking her to see him in his
office, but once she'd arrive, he would go off on long diatribes
about his ex-wife, his landlord hassles, his lack of money, barely mentioning her schoolwork. "The point, then, is that I *am*
dropping out of school, that I *am* getting married, and that I'm

really grateful to you for all your help."

"Fine." He was exhausted and had at least twelve more papers to grade. "Whatever makes you happy." He resented her even having come to see him; if he'd wanted to become a dean of students, he would have. "I think you'd have enjoyed graduate school. Despite a spotty high school background, you're developing a critical understanding, not only of works in isolation, but of literature in a larger context . . ." He sighed.

He'd always found her attractive, from the first sophomore survey class. Since the divorce, he'd dated a few of his students, as well as a teaching assistant in the theater department who, he soon discovered, was engaged, but she—despite informal lunches together—always kept things purely academic, listening to his professorial advice, heeding his words on study habits and critical texts, yet consistently refusing to reveal personal details (even during the few lunches when he'd had too much to drink and raved on about Deborah and Jason) making him, though he shuddered at the antiquated notion and what it revealed about himself, *respect* her. "Is something the matter?" he asked then. "Are you in trouble, or frightened about something?" Such abrupt intimacy embarrassed him.

"No."

Perhaps he detected a stifled laugh, perhaps not. He felt tired. There wasn't a single other student in his classes in the last year who had seemed so open to his subject; she'd appeared almost like a blue-jeaned tabula rasa in whom he'd been able to instill a passion for the written word, which had once, he recalled, been a passion of his own. Yet, he had to admit that all along he'd harbored occasional doubts as to her seriousness; if, like him, she'd had the opportunity to spend four cloistered and happy years on a grassy, thriving campus, working on a campus literary magazine, receiving praise from the dean, even the school president, away from the city and her family and the part-time clerical jobs. . . . His own school years were like fantasy: meeting Deborah during a school play, the evenings spent drinking, flirting, and philosophizing in the Graduate Club. Recently, he'd felt himself teaching by rote, mechanically reciting definitions for simile and metaphor, electing to teach only novels he wouldn't have to bother rereading. What more could he say to her? What more could be say to any of them? The sound of his own voice repelled him: once, during a class, in the middle of a lecture on Hemingway, he'd had to blink away tears.

He stood up, and she followed his lead. "Good luck," he said. They shook hands.

But then, as she was walking down the hall, he leaned out of his doorway to call, "It may not even be a mistake. It may be wonderful and in a few years you two will have enough money saved so that you'll come back and finish up . . . let's not lose touch . . . come back and visit . . ."

Her expression, as she turned around to stare at him, in the dimly lit halls of the makeshift "hut" which temporarily housed the English and speech departments until new quarters were established, was a cross, he decided, between cloudy and inscrutable.

This had been going on for a week. First she'd told her parents, then her brother in Baltimore, next her "overgrown guidance counselor," as she secretly thought of her therapist, and, finally, her professor. Now on her way to the subway, she'd run into two casual girlfriends (she had no close friends) from school, whom she supposed she ought to tell, also, when they asked her about her class schedule for the fall.

"Who is he?" one of them asked. "That guy you were looking at shoes with, when we ran into each other over break?"

"Oh, no. That was my brother. Someone else. You don't know him."

"What does he do?" asked the other.

"Lots of things, but nothing special, you know. He's trying to *find* himself . . . just like the rest of us. . . ."

Declining their invitation to have coffee, she entered the subway station, not caring which of the three lines she picked up. A local arrived first, and she rode it to 86th Street, then wandered into a Baskin-Robbins.

"Vanilla cone," she ordered, feeling a need to be inconspicuous; what she really wanted was one scoop of Rocky

Road, one scoop of Pralines n' Cream, with sprinkles and
nuts in a sugar cone, not this wafer cone with its pale vanilla scoop, but then people would have stared at her as she
walked along the streets, and some man would have been sure
to wisecrack as she struggled with her tongue to keep the two
colorful scoops upright, to keep the ice cream from dripping
all over the white tanktop and faded bluejeans.

She wasn't getting married. She had no boyfriend, no fiancé, no lover, no sweetheart, no honey, no steady beau: all of
the names for this thing she didn't have sounded delicious as
she walked along, biting into the cone. As her therapist knew,
she'd dated nobody since that time in Central Park when she'd
been left so alone; but what her therapist didn't know was how
she'd sat, alone on the bench, watching the faces of passersby
become the faces of ogres from suddenly recalled childhood
nightmares; watching the arms of an earring vendor become
writhing rattlesnakes, then cobras; watching the sun burn
itself out with wild red flames, and although she kept repeating her own name, first silently, then in whispers, and
touching her own rings and earrings and her eyes and nose
and mouth, finally she'd screamed. Later, in the emergency
room of the hospital, she'd telephoned her mother, who'd arrived quickly by taxi, crying and wearing a loose housedress,
to find her Thorazine-calmed daughter being questioned by
two policemen.

No, there would be no wedding, no honeymoon; what
there would be, instead, she thought, mocking her therapist,
was "self-actualization." She was actually going to do something all by herself; bored for too long now, annoyed by
the silly aspirations people continually declared hers, she
was simply going to leave, to change it all, at once, forever.
The detached amusement she'd felt each time that overgrown
high school guidance counselor with a master's degree would
talk to her about "getting better," or when her myopic professor, a man so obviously close to an edge, would imply that,
after a dissertation, she too would have the thrill of sitting in a
cubicle and circling grammatical errors, or when her mother
would tell a neighbor that her daughter didn't date because

she was "waiting for a nice boy," no longer existed; she felt hatred instead.

She was going to Boston. She would live in a Y, at first. She'd find a job. Her typing was what her employers labeled "decent"; her shorthand was less than that, and she'd once subbed for a switchboard operator. Certainly, she could compose business letters if asked. She did have some money saved from the summer and evening jobs, and even if it took a month to find work, she would scrimp on food and stay home each night.

Almost from the day after the Central Park incident, when her mother had begun speaking of her daughter's need for a good therapist, she'd been plotting out this trip. Boston was a city to which she'd been only once, for a weekend about three years before, to visit her mother's cousin who was dying of breast cancer. She remembered a shrunken, embittered woman of forty who'd looked eighty. And she remembered the waiting room of the Amtrak station, and some cobblestone streets and a large park, and a grocery store where they'd stopped for the sugarless fruit gum to which her mother jokingly confessed an addiction. Boston, like everywhere, was just a name. Travelling had consisted of the subways back and forth from her parents' apartment to high school, then college, and to the clerical jobs throughout; and, of course, the few childhood car trips to beaches in New Jersey and Connecticut, during which she'd become violently car sick, hating the red lights, which caused her father to step on the brakes and her stomach to churn, until, finally, at the second or third gas station to which she'd been taken to wash up, her irritated father would scream that he'd never, never take this Dramamine-immune daughter with him anywhere again. But now, at last, she was going to travel, like the other members of her generation, the ones she was continually seeing photos of in *Time* and *Newsweek*. A suitcase purchased on Orchard Street two weeks before was packed and waiting in a locker in Port Authority.

Even her parents believed she was getting married, both shedding tears over the fact that their future son-in-law was a

stranger to them, and that their daughter—always a problem
in one way or another—had chosen to be secretive, deceptive.
Her brother, attempting understanding long-distance from his
Baltimore apartment, sounded just as hurt: "Well, sweetheart,
you sure surprised *me*. I'd thought, since Michael, there hadn't
been any fellows . . ."

She'd promised her parents they would meet her fiancé
the coming weekend, and her mother had already asked twice
if he would prefer roast chicken and baked potatoes, or a tuna
casserole with a large salad, or possibly the chicken and salad;
but she'd be in Boston by the weekend, before her mother had
spent grocery money on the guest who would never arrive.
At some point, she'd write them. She wondered, just briefly,
how much pain she would cause. Really, she didn't believe
she wanted to cause them pain by her fabrication; they would
have been more hurt by an honest admission of her desire to
abandon everything. Well, perhaps she did desire vengeance
of a sort, but if so just a bit, and it didn't seem interesting
enough to analyze; that had been Mr. Master's Degree's job,
and he hadn't succeeded.

Port Authority was jammed. Her suitcase was waiting,
untouched (she'd feared all kinds of thieves and crazies) and
she replaced the key to the locker in its designated slot. The
ticket taker flirted with her, asking if she'd like to take along
a companion. She frowned, thinking how tired she was of
having men on the streets saying things to her, men on the
subways brushing against her as the cars swayed, men who
handed her change over the restaurant counters allowing their
fingers to linger too long, boys in her classes staring at her legs.
She'd be happy to become a secretary, at least for a while, in
Boston (a city she remembered—vaguely—as filled with staid,
taciturn, respectable New Englanders—men in spectacles and
tweed jackets, and women with short haircuts in belted tan
coats), earning a small salary, walking to and from her job
each day unnoticed, spending weekends alone at the movies. Her first apartment would be small but uncluttered, with
a Siamese cat named Hester, an Indian rug, a strong lamp and

a tall bookcase.

Waiting in line for the bus, she thought she noticed, heading toward another bus line (it was a Friday evening, and so not unlikely) her English professor. The glimpse was brief and the station was packed, but she was certain that the man wore the same beige trenchcoat and carried the same brown, sagging briefcase, and so she turned her head immediately in the opposite direction, although if it had been he, he'd already seen her, because he'd been staring (deliberately, it seemed to her) in her direction, and she was still in the same white tanktop and dungarees that she'd worn earlier in his office . . . but if it were he, he never came over to acknowledge her presence there in Port Authority, and she was able to step up, able to board the Greyhound bus undetected, feeling tidy and ready and not young at all, with two chunks of saran-wrapped cheese, an apple, a novel, and a cardigan sweater to slip over her shoulders in case she grew cold.

AMERICAN LOVE STORY

This is the sort of story that we believe should be passed from generation to generation, from quilt-making grannies to tow-headed little angels, from wizened, wiry grandpops to monkeyish lads. This isn't a bubble gum / muzak / supermarket-reading kind of love story: this isn't boy meets girl, then loses girl because: 1) blue eyes not bright enough, grinning molars not white enough; 2) boy's angry father thinks girl's parents not *his* kind of people; 3) girl's angry father thinks *boy's* parents not *his* kind of people; UNTIL! boy braves all obstacles, proves himself no longer boy but man, no longer pony but stallion, wins girl back, magnanimously forgives everyone else, and lives happily, sappily, forever after and even after that, if you know what we mean.

This story involves a boy, yes, a girl, yes, and also a car, a bird, a radio station, a tractor, the soil, a Dairy Queen, and in a sense, a cast of eight hundred and twenty-eight extras, the population of the town in which the boy and girl (hero and heroine if you choose, but we warn you that "hero" implies the perennially *good*, and there's no guarantee that in ten years from the time of this love story, the boy will not have grown into a man whose political or religious sensibilities offend you, with certain beliefs which you might not include in your personal realm of the *heroic*, and so we ask you to think twice before using those words, but your final decision remains personal) meet: in other words, this is a story of people during a specific time, owning and coveting specific things, living and working in specific places, because this is an American love story, and we are willing to eat our hats if this American love story doesn't have lasting telling power, if it doesn't warm more than a few little innocent hearts by more than a few blazing fireplaces for more than a few years to come.

The boy's name is Joseph, and he grew up on a farm, with a skinny, staunchly conservative father who owned an impressive collection of Roy Acuff records, a mother who enjoyed walking from room to room of her farmhouse, straightening paintings on the walls and doilies on the bureaus, a brother named Timothy, a brother named Stephen, a brother named Lester, and a sister named Georgette.

The girl's name was Lauren, and she had lived sixteen years, until the time of this story, on Lexington Avenue in New York City, in an apartment with a terrace which made you feel that if you reached out, stretched just a little more, and just a little bit more than *that*, you could touch the Empire State Building, and her building had elevators with piped-in music, and she had learned how to hail taxis on Fifth Avenue when she was eleven years old.

Lauren moved to Joseph's home town three years after her parents' divorce, when her mother's second husband was fired by a major radio station in New York City, and was only able to find an equivalently high position in a radio station in the middle of the country, in the middle of (as Lauren's mother described it) "nowhere." Lauren and her mother, Hedy, were both bitter and bewildered by the move (it's hard for us to figure out which of the two, at first, was more so, sixteen-year-old Lauren, who was used to snobbish private schools and had already once worked on a professional modeling assignment, or Hedy, who had never lived outside of a big city in her entire thirty-nine years, and who was addicted—*addicted!* she repeated—to certain New York department stores). "They'll mail you their catalogs," her second husband said dryly, because he had changed a bit during his bout with unemployment, had taken up running, had grown introspective, and had decided that he cared less about things like department stores and having a stepdaughter who was voted "best dressed" each year in her class.

Okay, hold it, you think, right there . . . so you're telling me another City Mouse, Country Mouse story . . . well, what's so special about that? We'll respond at once by asking you to think about yourself. If you're careful and honest, you'll face the fact that you're one or the other yourself. Either you love the subways, those subterranean, densely populated labyrinths which convince you that the whole planet consists of nothing but shooting black cars labeled by letter, which deposit you in underground circuses, or else you love the gnarled oak trees which remind you of the ones you scurried up as a child, and the chirping crickets which remind you of one particular summer out on the porch when the radio incessantly played a certain song by the Everly Brothers; either you can't bear to live without a staircase and a garden and the freedom to store your entire past in a large, dusty attic, or you wish for a one bedroom apartment across the street from an all-night cappuccino and pastry cafe. Oh, we concede that for brief periods of time—usually called, in the American Dream vocabulary—"vacations," you might convince yourself that you love both equally, but again, we'll simply and unceremoniously eat our hats if this is true. City Mouse or Country Mouse, take your pick and be proud.

Anyway, the City Mouse moved to the land of the Country Mouse at the time that this love story begins. Joseph was seventeen, a freshman majoring in business administration in the local college so that he could learn how to manage farms the modern, efficient, money-making way, and working from three until nine every day at Main Street's Dairy Queen, serving up floats, shakes, malts, burgers, fries, and onion rings.

Hedy, the mother of the City Mouse, is unfortunately a casualty of this story, and we'll feel better telling you that right out, now, before we become any more romantic. Hedy just stayed home all day ("It's not my home!" she insisted over and over), lethargically, not reading, not even watching television, thinking too often about her first husband, and looking too often in the mirror. She joined a tennis club and never went, registered for a class in flower arrangement and never attended.

But now the first true love affair of the story begins to unfold: Lauren and the yellow Subaru. Lauren had never been intimately involved with a car before. In the city she'd viewed all cars, in general, as the foreign objects New Jersey commuters drove in, parked in garages, and then drove out, but now she was madly in love with the Subaru's color, its sharp brakes, its sturdy tires, its grumblings while warming up, its AM radio, its purr. Lauren loved the fact that the Subaru spirited her away from her mother's blank face. She loved the way her own beautifully polished fingernails looked against the steering wheel, and the way the windshield wipers flicked away raindrops. Her stepfather took a series of photographs of her lounging, in various poses, astride and beside the car.

Joseph, too, had loves: he had a parrot (bought as an exotic gift by an uncle in Omaha) and he had the soil on his father's farm, and he loved helping out his father by riding the tractor whenever he had a chance, although lately he was too busy trying to maintain a B+ average and do a professional job at the Dairy Queen. Joseph also loved his dad's Roy Acuff collection, and he loved Hank Williams and Hank Williams, Jr. (He also had a girlfriend named Penny whom he'd known for years and liked a great deal, but minus magic, and he knew it.)

And the first warm afternoon that Lauren drove into the parking lot of the Main Street Dairy Queen (she'd been driving aimlessly for two hours and had gotten hungry) and pulled into a space beside a pick-up truck, walked inside and asked Joseph what flavor shakes he had, he fell in love with her, too. Lauren debated between vanilla and strawberry, figured that vanilla had less calories, and was ready to walk out once she'd counted her change.

Joseph took the deepest breath he'd ever taken. "Do you live around here?"

Cornball City, thought Lauren. "Yes," she said, and walked out.

That night, when Joseph's face kept running through Lauren's mind, she told herself, "I've dated a twenty-nine-year-old married photographer!" which was true, she had, the photographer who'd taken the pictures during her one modeling session, but the date had been the pits, he'd talked about his two-year-old daughter, and asked her how she liked chemistry, and reminisced about his own high school years. So what, she asked herself, had been the big deal.

Two weeks later when Lauren returned to the Dairy Queen, Joseph was behind the counter as she'd hoped, but he was leaning over and flirting with his girlfriend Penny as she played with a banana split. He paled, Lauren paled, and then Penny—who had once been extremely overweight and had remained insecure as a result, but who had coincidentally been thinking of breaking up with Joseph anyway, ever since her cousin had introduced her to a certain handsome theater major at school—also paled.

Lauren ordered onion rings in a shaking voice, but couldn't think of anything else to say, and Joseph's hands shook at the cash register, and Penny's chin turned hard, in a way that would eventually become habitual. This wasn't the sort of courtship Lauren was used to, but she was determined, and the next day she was back, circling until she found a space in the parking lot.

She stayed and sipped her shake until all the other customers had gone. Joseph felt calm, not surprised that she was waiting for him, and the fact that he'd received an 89 on an English exam earlier made him feel cocky. He asked her on a date.

That Friday night he arrived, and Lauren's stepfather beamed, pleased to see her socializing at last, while her mother stared blankly over their heads, concentrating upon some internal vista of her own.

Lauren was thrilled that he was in college, not still in high school, and she opened up and told him about how soon she had to make her own decision about where to apply, since she too had finished high school with excellent grades. They kissed in the movie theater, starting halfway through the first feature.

The next Friday night they went for pizza and then for a drive, this time in the Subaru, and they kissed and kissed again.

"I'm not a virgin," Lauren announced to Joseph, who never—even in his wildest dreams—would have brought up the subject. He was silent.

"Are you surprised?" Lauren asked. None of her sixteen-year-old friends were virgins; at least none admitted it. Each had had one boyfriend with whom she'd allowed passion to win. Lauren, in tenth grade, had dated a boy named Chris for seven months.

"Yes," admitted Joseph. "Since *I* am."

"I'm very lonely," said Lauren then. And she was, horribly lonely, lonelier than she'd ever been in her life, lonelier even than the day her own father had moved out and told her he'd call about getting together for dinner soon.

"But," said Joseph, "I don't have to stay one forever."

And that summer, their love bloomed. But we've decided not to elaborate too much upon certain sorts of details, not from prudery (we are *not* blushing!) but simply because *we* know that *you* know; there was nothing that Joseph, the Country Mouse, and Lauren, the City Mouse, did that summer that was any more special and lovely than what you once did during your first love affair, and what we, to be honest, once did during ours.

Wait just a minute, you sigh . . . a love story and you don't even want to supply the romantic details . . . what kind of a love story *is* this? The crux of the matter is in that very question, as it turns out, and we've already told you: this is a particularly *American* love story, one as much of things and places as boys and girls. The details we're discussing are different! Listen.

Lauren had to make her decision about college, and despite her love for Joseph, she applied to a prestigious school in a large city, and was accepted. And, of course, she and Joseph exchanged a few letters, but . . . In the meantime, Lauren's stepfather had fallen in love with the radio station and the town, but he and Hedy had fallen out of love with each other, and so during Lauren's Christmas and Easter vacations, she visited her mother back in New York City, where Hedy had chosen to return. Lauren's stepfather eventually married again, a public relations writer for the local bank, and they moved to a very old house with what neighbors called "a real history." Joseph graduated with high grades, fell in love with the daughter of a friend of his father's, married her and substantially increased profits on his father's farm. Penny dated the theater major for a while, but that broke up, and then she and her family moved away, and she was never able to overcome a certain resentment toward well-to-do women from large cities, although she herself married a well-to-do boy from Minneapolis, and lived with him there.

Because of Joseph and the Subaru, Lauren remembers her stay in that small town with affection; Joseph feels pleased that his first sexual experiences were with such a kind, generous teacher.

This American love story, you can see, involves the things we all know and love well: cars and fast foods and early sex and divorce and marriage and maybe even a little adultery (there was a rumor, we might as well tell you, about Lauren's stepfather and a secretary at the radio station) and high school and college and high grades on tests and farms and cities and taxis and careers and apartments and houses and packing up all one's wordly goods and moving vans and packing up again and moving vans again and packing up and moving on again and again.

We tell you this story, we insist, so that the women of today growing into the grandmothers of tomorrow, and the men of today growing into delightful old codgers, will have a story to sit back and slowly deliver with embellishments, one that reflects who they are, and were, and will be: no Victorian prudery, no Gothic haunted houses, no mysterious counts and countesses. We give to you, so that you may give to your grandchildren and great-grandchildren, a story at once tangible, mobile, and honest: a love story about the people we really love best.

CITY LIGHTS PUBLICATIONS

Angulo de, Jaime. INDIANS IN OVERALLS
Angulo de, J. and G. de Angulo. JAIME IN TAOS
Antler, FACTORY
Artaud, Antonin. ARTAUD ANTHOLOGY
Bataille, Georges. EROTISM: Death and Sensuality
Bataille, Georges. STORY OF THE EYE
Bataille, Georges. THE TEARS OF EROS
Baudelaire, Charles. INTIMATE JOURNALS
Baudelaire, Charles. TWENTY PROSE POEMS
Bowles, Paul. A HUNDRED CAMELS IN THE COURTYARD
Brecht, Stefan. POEMS
Broughton, James. SEEING THE LIGHT
Bukowski, Charles. THE MOST BEAUTIFUL WOMAN IN TOWN
Bukowski, Charles. TALES OF ORDINARY MADNESS
Bukowski, Charles. NOTES OF A DIRTY OLD MAN
Burroughs, William S. THE BURROUGHS FILE
Burroughs, William S. THE YAGE LETTERS
Cardenal, Ernesto. FROM NICARAGUA WITH LOVE
Carrington, Leonora. THE HEARING TRUMPET
Cassady, Neal. THE FIRST THIRD
Choukri, Mohamed. FOR BREAD ALONE
CITY LIGHTS REVIEW #1: Formalist Avant-gardes issue
CITY LIGHTS REVIEW #2: Forum on AIDS & the Arts issue
CITY LIGHTS REVIEW #3: Forum on Media and Propaganda issue
Cocteau, Jean. THE WHITE BOOK (LE LIVRE BLANC)
Codrescu, Andrei, ed. EXQUISITE CORPSE READER
Cornford, Adam. ANIMATIONS
Corso, Gregory. GASOLINE
David-Neel, Alexandra. SECRET ORAL TEACHINGS IN TIBETAN
    BUDDHIST SECTS
Deleuze, Gilles. SPINOZA: PRACTICAL PHILOSOPHY
Dick, Leslie. WITHOUT FALLING
di Prima, Diane. PIECES OF A SONG: Selected Poems
Ducornet, Rikki. ENTERING FIRE
Duras, Marguerite. MARGUERITE DURAS
Eidus, Janice. VITO LOVES GERALDINE
Eberhardt, Isabelle. THE OBLIVION SEEKERS
Fenollosa, Ernest. THE CHINESE WRITTEN CHARACTER
    AS A MEDIUM FOR POETRY
Ferlinghetti, Lawrence. LEAVES OF LIFE
Ferlinghetti, Lawrence. PICTURES OF THE GONE WORLD
Ferlinghetti, Lawrence. SEVEN DAYS IN NICARAGUA LIBRE
Franzen, Cola, transl. POEMS OF ARAB ANDALUSIA
García Lorca, Federico. ODE TO WALT WHITMAN & OTHER POEMS
García Lorca, Federico. POEM OF THE DEEP SONG
Gascoyne, David. A SHORT SURVEY OF SURREALISM
Ginsberg, Allen. HOWL & OTHER POEMS
Ginsberg, Allen. KADDISH & OTHER POEMS
Ginsberg, Allen. REALITY SANDWICHES
Ginsberg, Allen. PLANET NEWS
Ginsberg, Allen. THE FALL OF AMERICA
Ginsberg, Allen. MIND BREATHS
Ginsberg, Allen. PLUTONIAN ODE

Goethe, J. W. von. TALES FOR TRANSFORMATION
H.D. (Hilda Doolittle). NOTES ON THOUGHT & VISION
Hayton-Keeva, Sally, ed. VALIANT WOMEN IN WAR AND EXILE
Herron, Don. THE LITERARY WORLD OF SAN FRANCISCO
Higman, Perry, transl. LOVE POEMS FROM SPAIN AND SPANISH AMERICA
Jaffe, Harold. EROS (In the Time of AIDS)
Kerouac, Jack. BOOK OF DREAMS
Kerouac, Jack. SCATTERED POEMS
Kovic, Ron. AROUND THE WORLD IN 8 DAYS
Lacarrière, Jacques. THE GNOSTICS
La Duke, Betty. COMPANERAS: Women, Art & Social Change in Latin America
La Loca, ADVENTURES ON THE ISLE OF ADOLESCENCE
Lamantia, Philip. MEADOWLARK WEST
Lamantia, Philip. BECOMING VISIBLE
Laughlin, James. THE MASTER OF THOSE WHO KNOW
Laughlin, James. SELECTED POEMS: 1935-1985
Low, Mary and Juan Breá. RED SPANISH NOTEBOOK
Lowry, Malcolm. SELECTED POEMS
Marcelin, Philippe-Thoby. THE BEAST OF THE HAITIAN HILLS
Masereel, Frans. PASSIONATE JOURNEY
McDonough, Kaye. ZELDA
Moore, Daniel. BURNT HEART
Mrabet, Mohammed. THE BOY WHO SET THE FIRE
Mrabet, Mohammed. THE LEMON
Mrabet, Mohammed. LOVE WITH A FEW HAIRS
Mrabet, Mohammed. M'HASHISH
Murguía, A. & B. Paschke, eds. VOLCAN: Poems from Central America
O'Hara, Frank. LUNCH POEMS
Olson, Charles. CALL ME ISHMAEL
Paschke, B. & D. Volpendesta, eds. CLAMOR OF INNOCENCE
Pessoa, Fernando. ALWAYS ASTONISHED
Pasolini, Pier Paolo. ROMAN POEMS
Poe, Edgar Allan. THE UNKNOWN POE
Porta, Antonio. KISSES FROM ANOTHER DREAM
Purdy, James. IN A SHALLOW GRAVE
Purdy, James. GARMENTS THE LIVING WEAR
Prévert, Jacques. PAROLES
Rey-Rosa, Rodrigo. THE BEGGAR'S KNIFE
Rigaud, Milo. SECRETS OF VOODOO
Rips, Geoffrey, ed. UNAMERICAN ACTIVITIES
Saadawi El, Nawal. MEMOIRS OF A WOMAN DOCTOR
Sawyer-Lauçanno, Christopher, transl. THE DESTRUCTION OF THE JAGUAR
Sclauzero, Mariarosa. MARLENE
Serge, Victor. RESISTANCE
Shepard, Sam. MOTEL CHRONICLES
Shepard, Sam. FOOL FOR LOVE & THE SAD LAMENT OF PECOS BILL
Smith, Michael. IT A COME
Snyder, Gary. THE OLD WAYS
Solomon, Carl. MISHAPS PERHAPS
Tutuola, Amos. FEATHER WOMAN OF THE JUNGLE
Tutuola, Amos. SIMBI & THE SATYR OF THE DARK JUNGLE
Valaoritis, Nanos. MY AFTERLIFE GUARANTEED
Waley, Arthur. THE NINE SONGS
Wilson, Colin. POETRY AND MYSTICISM